A VAMPIRE AND SERIAL KILL[

BLOOD

TRISH

BOOK 1

K.T. ROSE

CW01498710

Blood
Trish: A Vampire and Serial Killer Thriller Series, Book 1

Copyright © 2025 by Kyrobooks

All rights reserved.

The characters and incidents mentioned in this publication are entirely fictional.

The transmission, duplication, or reproduction of any of the following work, including specific information, will be considered an illegal act irrespective of if it is done electronically or in print. This extends to creating a secondary or tertiary copy of the work or a recorded copy and is only allowed with expressed written consent from the Publisher. All additional right reserved.

Written by: K.T. Rose
Cover Design: Cha

ABOUT THE AUTHOR

K.T. Rose is a horror, thriller, supernatural, paranormal, and suspense author based in Detroit, Michigan. She shares her passion for spine-chilling stories with readers through flash fiction on her blog. Her works include *Trinity of Horror*, *The Haunting of Gallagher Hotel*, the *Netted* Series, and *The Trish Vampire and Serial Killer Thriller* Series.

Hunger. Desperation. Terror. A mother's love knows no bounds—neither does her appetite.

A vampire's existence is a delicate balance between predator and pretense. For Trish, that balance includes a loving husband, an innocent son, and a trail of bloodless corpses. When her latest hunt at Miller University goes awry, leaving a witness in its wake, her carefully maintained double life begins to crumble.

Months later, Trish sets her sights on a pure-hearted professor, but his death brings unexpected consequences. Captured by the victim's vengeful cousin and her violent friends, Trish faces a harrowing choice. She must either break free to protect her family or watch her perfect life dissolve into chaos. Can she escape before her husband, Randel, discovers the true nature of the monster he married?

Blood introduces K.T. Rose's chilling vampire horror thriller series. If you're drawn to dark supernatural tales, complex characters, and blood-chilling suspense, this story of maternal instinct versus monster nature will leave you breathless.

CONTENTS

About the Author iii

Part 1: Miller University, August 2024
Chapter 1: Chad 3
Chapter 2: Prying Eyes 7

Part 2: Two Months Later
Chapter 3: Mrs. Mom 13
Chapter 4: Baby 17
Chapter 5: Daycare 21
Chapter 6: Thirty-Seven 28

Part 3: Sweet Home, West Virginia
Chapter 7: 1889 37
Chapter 8: Grown Up 47
Chapter 9: The Coop 50
Chapter 10: Friends and Neighbors 55

Part 4: Preparations
Chapter 11: Maggie 63
Chapter 12: Southern Luna 68
Chapter 13: Storage 73
Chapter 14: Miller, MI 78
Chapter 15: Young's Bar and Grill 82
Chapter 16: Locals 86
Chapter 17: Toby 90

Chapter 18: Doubt 95
Chapter 19: Ride 98

Part 5: Blood Lust
Chapter 20: The Preacher's House 105
Chapter 21: Feast..112
Chapter 22: Barbie and the Gents...116
Chapter 23: Blood 120
Chapter 24: Chained Up 124
Chapter 25: Junk 128
Chapter 26: Ol' Blue Eyes...134
Chapter 27: Window 143
Chapter 28: Slippery Fingers..148
Chapter 29: Stay 151

Part 6: Monster
Chapter 30: Death of a Monster 159
Chapter 31: Steps...162
Chapter 32: The Kitchen 166
Chapter 33: The Barrel 172
Chapter 34: Escape 177
Chapter 35: Questions 182

Part 7: Homebound
Chapter 36: A New Crisis 193
Chapter 37: Wheelbarrow Wheels 196
Chapter 38: Bath 200
Chapter 39: Gold..206
Chapter 40: Paranoia 212
Chapter 41: Existence 217

Excerpt From Books 2: Monster...223
More from K.T. Rose 231

PART 1

Miller University, August 2024

CHAPTER 1

Chad

Trish wasn't a student at Miller University. In fact, she went to Radcliffe before women were allowed to take Havard classes. No, she was at Miller with a different purpose in mind, and it had nothing to do with studying. She was sitting in some frat boy's dorm room—Chad was his name—with her fangs deep in his wrist, sucking on his musky skin and careful to lick up the mess of blood that ran from the wound like water leaking from a faucet. She considered the meal subpar; it was a little too sweet for her taste. Chad had certainly eaten nothing but cookies and Jello shots all day, skipping protein and salt. Luckily, human blood naturally had enough protein and salt in each sip; Chad would sustain her for a month. Lightheaded and intertwined in gluttonous bliss, her body swayed with delight as she took him in.

Chad twitched at the shoulders as he lay on the extra-long twin bed, his body limp and lacking the oxygen needed for consciousness, let alone enough to put up a fight. Trish figured that he had been about twenty-one years old. He was tall enough to play sports, and his build was fair with a little weight around his middle. His face was empty of wrinkles, young and new, and his smile was pearly. Chad had taken the time to chat her up before they headed to his room. He said something about playing an instrument and liking computers. He certainly told the truth about that, judging by the black trombone case leaning against a desk with the biggest monitors she'd ever seen sitting on top of it. The room's small size—slightly larger than a walk-in closet—made the computer look enormous. She was surprised the tiny room possessed a closet. To keep the conversation going, she pretended to be intrigued as she shared some lies about herself. She couldn't remember if she was Julie from the accounting firm or Tiffany from the dealership. It didn't matter. Her meals' backstories seem to run together anyway, making it hard for her to put hobbies, jobs, and names with the faces of the corpses in her wake. As she and Chad stood toe to toe at the party downstairs, the only thing she thought of was his sweaty pores; the chemical scent of alcohol still wafted from him as he lay on his bed dying. Trish hated the smell, but it signified easy prey, like most college boys, truckers, or, in desperate times, a person down on their luck left to dig through pub and restaurant dumpsters. They were all so easy to trap and drain.

Trish caressed the edges of the lacerations on Chad's arm with her tongue, pushing his blood to flow into her mouth as the party raged on beneath her feet. The attendees roared and chanted, yelled for more beer, and demanded someone to take their shirt off. The voices were the familiar sounds of the naïve—too drunk and high on acid or pot to notice there was a monster upstairs.

Sometimes, Trish wondered if college students' parents bothered to teach them the basics; namely, not to bring strange women into their rooms. But, no matter how thin and pale she looked in that dark dress, men always fell for her. Her lean figure and plump lips were effective bait—irresistibly mysterious, she was told. Still, when the police found their bodies, there was always mourning and a sense of loss for someone so young and talented. Someone that human society classified as potentially important. Chad believed that hype, having told her that he was working on a chemical engineering degree and minoring in music. He was *so close* to graduating and living *that* life. As he spoke, Trish pictured him getting married to some nurse, buying a house, and having kids, because that's what humans did. But what Chad didn't know—a tidbit that she decided to keep to herself—was that he was doomed to become an unhappy, overworked middle manager who flirted with the idea of sticking a barrel in his mouth. She'd seen many people like him over the last one

4

hundred and thirty-seven years. Chad was a cliché; there was nothing special about his dreams because he wouldn't live long enough to loathe them. In fact, Chad had done Trish a favor by curing her cramps and insufferable hunger pains, and for that, she was grateful.

Chad stopped jerking, and her belly was full. She slowly withdrew her fangs, allowing blood to drip onto her lap. She used one hand to get a tight grip on his arm, forming a tourniquet. There was no pulse, just as she expected. With her free hand, she pulled the pocketknife from her leather tote, which lay against her thigh.

Trish learned a long time ago that a murder could be hidden in plain sight. By the time prey was found, their bodies would bleed out from the wrist or the neck. It could be suicide. It could be murder. The police never really knew. Even though she had to leave Chad in his bed for everyone to find, she preferred getting rid of the corpse by burying it somewhere *massive* like the ocean, the lake, a construction site…a dump. She'd make the authorities look for months, years, decades, then wash her hands of the situation, because if they did find the body, there was no DNA—the biological code they used to match a crime with a killer.

She pulled the blade up Chad's wrist, along her fang marks. The knife tore his skin in half and flooded the wound with his leftover liquids. His blood had gone syrupy and thick, tempting her to lick it dry. But it was close to clotting; it would taste bitter and have all the consistency of old, clumpy cottage cheese.

Trish laid Chad's arm on his bed and considered his pale face. He was a different person from the man she made out with and strangled before she went in for the kill. His eyelids were at half-mast and he seemed peaceful.

She unclenched his fingers and dipped them into the new gash. Then she slid the knife into his palm, staging his body.

Then she listened. She listened *hard* and kicked herself for not doing so sooner. She didn't think straight, or at all, when she was hungry, and Chad seemed reserved—she was sure that his room was empty and that no one knew about the woman that he allowed upstairs. He'd even locked the door behind them. During her quick survey upon entry, she didn't see anything. As they huffed and made out, swapped tongues and giggled, she didn't hear anything alarming. And as she subdued him and slurped his blood, she didn't smell anyone.

But right then was the crucial time to listen and engross herself in her environment because she was done eating. It was time to leave unnoticed because anything could happen around *them*. Them, meaning humans. Them, meaning blood bags. Them, meaning food…

Trish heard a young girl vomiting outside, just below the window. She imagined it smelled like cheap vodka and tapas. The boys just beneath her feet slammed shots of what smelled like pure ethanol. A girl bawled her eyes out just next door as she yelled about how someone was a horrible boyfriend.

And then Trish heard heavy breathing in the closet. The hairs on her neck rose.

CHAPTER 2

Prying Eyes

Trish stood, eyes trained on the closet door. It was light brown with a golden knob, and someone was hiding behind it. For a second, she wondered if her own senses were going with age. How had she not noticed before? She knew about all the noises and smells, and it could be hard to isolate a sound or a scent. But it hadn't always been *that* hard.

Humans smelled like iron and body odor, and she was surrounded by them. But she missed the one that was right under her nose. Not the one who lay dead on his bed, but the one that was hiding in his closet. Whoever was on the other side had been quiet for a long time as they watched the monster work.

She narrowed her eyes and approached slowly. Her mellow legs threatened to sit her back down as her full belly pleaded for time to digest. Her claws extended, scraping the nail beds of her fingers as they grew out to the length of full-sized steak knives. Her fingers bled as her body went on the defense. The breaths on the other side of the door quickened, and with a drunken, hurried stride, Trish grabbed the doorknob and snatched the door open.

Someone, a young woman, rushed Trish, shoving her in the gut with her shoulder. Trish fell back toward the bed and onto Chad. She felt light on her feet and in her head, tottering in awe. The short, skinny girl overpowered her, but only for a second.

The girl sprang for the door, shouting, "Help!" Her deep bronze skin was even and soft, young and beautiful. But her hazel eyes were full of alarm and terror, and when she darted past, a whiff of sweet wine (*tropical? fruit punch?*) hit Trish in the face. That was it. That's how Trish missed her. The girl's scent blended with everyone else's, including the very dead, once very drunk Chad. But full or not, high off blood or not, Trish couldn't let her get away.

Springing for her, and nearly collapsing under her own clumsy weight, Trish snatched the girl by her long, thick, crinkly hair. She yanked, pulling the girl back and bringing her ear to Trish's mouth. There was no time to find a place to make her disappear. Trish had to drain her right then and there. Already bloated, blurry-eyed, and lethargic, she barely had room for dessert. But she was going to *make* room.

She planted her free hand on the girl's mouth and embedded her claws into her cheeks, careful not to draw blood. "You like to sneak around?" Trish asked softly.

The girl tried to scream underneath Trish's hand.

"Shut up and listen," Trish quipped through bared teeth.

The girl's heart slammed hard in her chest; her blood pressure was out of whack. A high blood pressure meant big red messes that screamed *murder*. No real investigation required. There wasn't enough time to clean or subdue the girl because of her clear outburst—a desperate call for *help*. Someone had to have heard it.

The girl tried shouting again, and Trish considered crushing her face with her tightening grip. *Nah. That'll leave an even bigger mess*, she thought. Instead, Trish said, "Look, I don't know why you were in that closet, but you just saw the last thing you'll ever see."

The girl jerked and wiggled, fighting hard to break free, but Trish was stronger. Trish was *always* stronger, full or not. She stuck her fangs into the girl's neck, forcing her to squirm. Trish closed her eyes, enjoying the taste—the blood was better than the dead boy's on the bed. The girl had drunk some alcohol, but not as much as Chad had. Yeah, she smoked some weed, the slight earthy tinge of THC lingering within her life liquid said as much, but she ate sweeteners.

Not candy and ice cream, but fruits and vegetables. Tea and honey. She was healthy. A perfect dessert.

The girl's blood cascaded down Trish's throat, elevating her mind and body to a celestial high. She gorged on sweet nectar, seeing double as she opened her eyes and watched the door split and collide, playing tricks with her vision. The girl twisted and turned, weakened against Trish's grip until she went limp.

"Hmmmm," Trish hummed, pleased. Another win. Another meal. Another…

"Hey, Chad!" Banging on the door from the opposite side. Trish slowed down to listen, hoping that her mind was still playing tricks on her as it embraced her new trip, flipping the sense of her surroundings to autopilot, leaving all control to her need to feed. "Chad! Everything all right in there?" a man cried.

She gulped down a mouth full of blood and her breath caught in her chest. The voice on the other side of the door was very real. With that, she frantically drank and sucked. *Come on, come on,* Trish thought. The girl's heart was still pumping even though she was unconscious. If Trish stopped, the girl may turn into a monster, just as Trish had turned all those years ago. *Four more minutes,* Trish thought as her actual allotted time shrunk to almost nothing.

"No, I *know* something's wrong." The voice of a girl on the other side of the door. "I heard a big banging noise and someone shouting for help. I heard it from the bathroom, and it came from *in there.*"

Dammit, Trish thought as she continued to suck in blood.

The banging on the door again. "Chad! Open the door!" a man shouted.

No. No. Shit! She swallowed, gulping blood as fast as her throat would allow.

Heavy thuds on the door erupted as if two guys were slamming their linebacker shoulders into it.

With her fangs still buried in the girl's throat, she dragged them, slicing her prey's jugular in half, slitting the girl's neck. Blood splashed Trish's face as she pulled her fangs free and dropped the girl, whose neck was gushing blood as if she had taken a machete to the throat. Her body slammed against the carpet.

Feeling drugged, Trish snatched up her purse and sprinted for the window. She slid it open and stepped out onto the shingled roof and hopped down into a thick brush alongside the house.

A scream rang out into the night from the second floor as she crouched in the brush, using her arm to swipe blood from her face. She did not bother looking up, because she was sure the guys were looking down, searching for the perpetrator.

As she crawled on her knees, picking up pebbles and wood-chips, she hoped the girl was dead. She hoped her fang marks looked more like cuts or slits, not teeth. *Oh shit, shit, shit,* she thought, her nerves racing as her bare knees slammed into the ground and she struggled to beat her own shadow.

Once she found an opening in the brush where it appeared clear on the opposite side of the house and away from the crowded entrance, she broke through the tall sticky shrubs and ran, her pumps clipping the concrete as she pushed her way through kids coming from or going to one of the many parties happening that night. They didn't mind her, and she blended with them. Still, she didn't look or notice if anyone had seen her because it didn't matter if there was blood on her face. It didn't matter if none of them recognized her from any of her classes. It didn't matter that she had just killed two people—they would never find her.

They never do.

PART 2

Two Months Later

CHAPTER 3

Mrs. Mom

"Trish?" Randel's soft whisper tickled her ear, making her warm inside.

His mere presence allowed her to believe she was normal, and she accepted it with a smile. The quiet bedroom was still around them, allowing her to listen to her steady heartbeat, though she barely ever slept. She opened her eyes, blinking slowly and adjusting to the darkness.

"Trish?" Randel sang, his breath gentle against her cheek.

Euphoria embraced her soul, somehow putting her at ease all over again, just as it had every morning when she awoke next to him.

Trish groaned playfully and turned on her side to face him. She couldn't find his eyes, but she knew he was there with his silky dark bed hair, and tanned body bare of everything but briefs. Trish threw her arm over his hip, finding it exposed. He groaned, and she giggled, further comforted by the sincere notion. She silently cherished that security, and she floated on air, feeling his body in the dark. Trish lifted her hand and found his face, running her fingers through his silky hair. His lips met hers, and she basked in a glow of emotional bliss. He made her feel human again—wholeheartedly, not just partly.

Randel gave her a reason to *feel*. If she could, she'd dump whatever remained of her soul in his lap and allow him to work his magic, bringing her back to life. But that wasn't her reality, although it was very much his.

She strained to see his face, longing to gaze at the most intriguing man she'd ever encountered. He was so different from the others. From the way his deep voice made her heart bloom, to his skin that shined golden in the burning sun, or the cute dimple on his chiseled chin. His charm was unpredictable, drawing neighbors and friends like hummingbirds to honeysuckle.

"Honey, it's your turn," he said. His words were easy and calm.

"For what?"

"What do you think?" he asked.

Then, she *heard* what—Darwin was crying in the next room.

Trish sniffed and wiped tiredness from another deep meditative night from her eyes, then sighed, allowing the full volume of Darwin's cries to settle deep in her ears. Even though the boy was one-year-old, he still didn't seem to care about sleeping. Darwin was her and Randel's personal alarm clock: waking Randel for work and Trish for mommy duty.

She envied them for their ability to reach level two of the sleep cycle. Earlier on, it had been difficult to handle whenever she was in her human form. However, over time, her topical experience with rest only turned into deep meditation. It was the only time where her consciousness remained on autopilot—a place where she loosened her grip on reality and relaxed for a few hours.

Trish threw the thick comforter off her body and went to stand up. But before she left the bed, Randel sprang for her and pulled her close, hugging her from behind. His broad, bare chest pressed against her back. He planted his lips against her neck and wrapped his arms around her tightly. Then he reached for her hands and wrapped his big fingers around hers, placing them on either side of the base of her ring finger, flicking around the wedding ring he'd bought.

With the warm feeling of pleasure depleted, she cringed, hating him for touching it. The three-stone, tapered diamond ring he'd bought her had to have cost over six thousand dollars. It was pretty and fine, glinting and expensive. A ring most girls would strive for. But it served another purpose, one she didn't want him touching for fear of the middle diamond falling out as it concealed her lifeline that filled the inner white-gold walls.

Randel could never know that.

But if he found out... Trish contemplated this, her stomach rumbling with the onslaught of morning hunger pains. So, she only lay there because there was no way to stop him without raising suspicion and prompting him to become Mr. Interrogation. Not only was Randel a decent parent and lover, a wonderful son and constantly climbing the ladder at Haven Software Consultants, he was good at digging pointless rabbit holes that she'd have to bury in real time.

Trish sighed. How would she answer his questions? She couldn't, and she didn't. So Randel continued caressing the wedding ring, something unique to him and him alone.

Each of her husbands had been different, and the rings they'd put on her finger showed that. They'd been of a similar caliber—silver or gold. Diamonds, rubies, or sapphires. Every man's style was infused in their choice of ring. But no matter the style, the stone, or the cost, those rings served the same purpose that had always outlived the man who bought it.

No matter how important the piece of jewelry was, they *never* caressed it. They never spun it around her finger or tugged at it. They never hummed happily as they touched it. But Randel always did.

"Go take care of our kid, Wife," he whispered.

Trish chuckled and pulled away from him, thankful for the way out. She planted her bare feet on the shaggy rug and headed for the robe hanging on the back of the closet door. "I love you, you know that?" she said. "Even though you're a lazy turd."

"Me? Lazy? *Nah*," he said playfully.

"Yeah, yeah, it's really *your* turn, and you know it. But since I'm an amazing mom, I'll bow out of this fight graciously."

"Oh, well, how graceful of you," he rasped as he turned away, burying himself in the comforter.

After pulling the silk robe over her shoulders and fastening it around her waist, Trish headed for the nightstand and picked up her phone: 5:48 a.m.

She cocked her head with a half-smile. *At least Darwin's waiting a little later to cry*, she thought, silently celebrating a major stride in understanding her baby. It was the first of many things she wished to understand. Darwin's sleep schedule alternated from sporadic naps to a solid five-to-six-hour night. She'd silently agreed to take his wake-up calls any day, so long as they were after 5 a.m. and before 11 p.m.

CHAPTER 4

Baby

Legs stiff and eyes low, Trish trudged across the hall, watching the dim blue glow on the floor just in front of Darwin's room. His favorite nightlight was hard at work, just like it had been most nights.

Are babies afraid of the dark? she thought. *Do they even know what fear is?* Trish would never know; he wasn't capable of holding a full conversation outside of his casual, slobbery baby babble.

When she was pregnant, she was sure he'd be a night owl like her. She remembered the days when Darwin kicked at her insides and pressed against the wall of her uterus. At night he was more aggressive, his little kicks harder, and his little hand pressed outward as if he would make his own way out.

Also, he preferred eating at night, which didn't bother her as much. In fact, she enjoyed it because she got to eat animal meat and fruit without having to vomit or deal with a prolonged spout of nausea. They ate pistachios and strawberry ice cream while laughing at funny videos.

However, once he was born, she regretted her pregnancy diet. Her body ached and the debilitating pain put her out of commission for a week; that was, until she went out into the city and killed a young woman. In fact, after her pregnancy, she no longer required a body once a season as she always had. She needed to eat monthly, quickly becoming responsible for a sizable portion of the missing persons lists in Indiana, Ohio, Illinois, and, of course, her home state of Michigan.

Trish found Darwin standing, his back straight and his plump hands wrapped tightly around the oak railing of his baby bed. He was handsome like Randel, down to his tanned skin and dark eyes. He pulled aggressively, making the crib beneath him shiver in response. Darwin bent his knees and bounced with a flustered grunt. His dark eyes pouted, and tears poured down his slick face. He griped, as if yelling, *Hurry, Ma!* She yawned. "I'm coming, kiddo." She rubbed his soft, black hair, then picked him up. Instantly, he began climbing up her torso as she coddled him. She smiled and peered down at his bed, looking for his bottle. Clouds and a happy sun smiled at them from his carousel.

"Hm," she said.

His bottle wasn't there, and some pieces of the carousel were missing.

As the carousel spun slowly, a gap stood where a cloud had been, and opposite that, a star was missing too. Trish searched around the floor, holding the squirming boy. His navy rug with a white crescent moon sat in the middle of the room. The moon smiled with its eyes closed. Human-sized teddy bears lined the opposite wall near the door: the smiling grizzly bear Trish had gotten him from her trip to Indiana and a light blue bunny his Nana Shannon, Randel's mom, had gotten him for Easter.

Trish scoffed; human holidays were silly. She contemplated throwing the toy away and raising her son as an atheist or simply someone who didn't blame or cherish a faux higher power, but Randel was against it.

"I love you no matter what your beliefs are, but my family is Catholic, and so is Darwin," Randel had declared a few weeks before Darwin was born.

Trish looked along the wall next to the teddy bears and two toy boxes, one shaped like a wooden wagon and another with a yellow rhino on the side of it. Still, there was no sign of the bottle or the carousel parts.

She sighed. "Where did you put your stuff, crazy child?" Trish searched around the oak changing station and the wicker dirty clothes basket. Everything was neat and in place.

Darwin continued fussing, turning his little body and waving his chunky arms. "Fine, fine, fine," she said, deciding to continue her search later.

"Hungry?" she asked him, not expecting a clear answer.

He growled in response. Then he said, "Ewww." The only word that he seemed to know and repeat for about two weeks. Everything warranted a scowl and an *ewwww* from the kid. Shopping trip? *Ew.* Food? *Ew.* Daycare? *Ew.* Daddy? *Ew.*

"Ewwww *you*, pumpkin," she teased, but he didn't stop digging his small toes into her torso and tightening his arms around her neck. The unfamiliar pressure of Darwin's bear hug made Trish's throat tighten. "Darwin," she said, "you're choking Mommy."

Darwin released his grip and tossed his head back, going limp. But his cries didn't cease. In fact, he screamed and kicked.

"Well, someone's in a dramatic mood."

She hauled the baby down the steps which led to the kitchen. Trish pulled the fridge open and grabbed the fresh bottle sitting on the top shelf, just in front of the pot roast and the red potatoes Randel had roasted the night before. She spun, using her foot to close the refrigerator, as little Darwin reached for the bottle, clutching his fingers into a fist, then opening them as if to say, *Gimme.*

"All right, all right," Trish said with a smile.

She handed him the bottle and chuckled when he snatched it. He shoved the clear nipple into his mouth and scarfed the cold formula down. She watched him suck it dry, a lot like she had been doing with her own food lately. Trish couldn't help it. Just like Darwin and anyone else, *human* or *beast*, they all had to eat. Her condition came with some regrets. For instance, she hated feeding Darwin formula. Since he was born, Trish felt the boy deserved the best—what good parents didn't feel that way? He deserved food from a natural source—nutrition and nourishment from Mommy. Randel's guilt trip on unhealthy chemicals and missing the *human connection* played out in her mind word for word every time she fed Darwin.

But she could not give their son that type of care and she'd never tell her husband why. She'd never tell *anyone* why. To make up for such a disconnection, she gave Darwin gluten-free baby food and only fed him from glass bottles. It was the equivalent of eating beluga lentils caviar from a sterling silver spoon. That's the kind of shit people cared about in that century—at least, that's what the internet told her.

It isn't like Darwin has a choice, Trish thought.

She looked down at him. The boy appeared to be clenching his jaws, holding a tight-gummed smile as his dark eyes stared into hers.

"Done?" she asked.

He jumbled his legs, doing his happy dance.

Trish pulled the empty bottle away and set it on the kitchen table.

"Burpy time," she announced, placing the child over her shoulder and patting his back.

He buried his face in her neck.

"Ow!" she yelped as his small teeth clamped down on her skin and a sharp pang tore through her neck.

Darwin giggled once he let go.

"Dammit, pumpkin, that hurts!" she shouted, putting her hand over the bite. Trish held her fingers out, searching. No blood.

For a second, she was sure he'd pierced her neck. Astounded, she rubbed her finger over the wet spot again and found nothing but baby spit.

CHAPTER 5

Daycare

"You guys having fun in here?" Randel asked as he went for the coffeemaker on the granite countertop. He finally rolled out of bed and was wearing a white tank top and red flannel pajama bottoms. He picked up the glass pot and filled it with water from the sink. Then he rubbed his fresh-shaven chin as he poured the water into the coffeemaker.

"Sure," Trish said. She went up to the kitchen table, pulled Darwin's highchair tabletop off, and sat him there.

Darwin slammed his hands down on his tabletop after she secured it. He frowned and grumbled, as if he was imprisoned in his chair. His wailing went on until she returned with a box of Grain Ohs and poured a few onto his tabletop.

As she rubbed her stinging neck, Randel said, "You know that cereal will end up on the floor. They're like toys to him." He pulled the lid off the coffee container, and Trish felt her stomach twist at the engrossing scent of bitter coffee beans.

"Stopped him from crying, didn't it?" she said, opting to stay near the table with Darwin over being in the midst of the coffee making, even though it didn't seem to matter. The smell had taken over the house.

After getting the coffee pot started, Randel reached for her and kissed her on the lips. He hugged her, and she buried her face in his chest as he rubbed the length of her body. She smiled, preferring his sweet cologne over the strong coffee beans any day.

She looked over her shoulder at Darwin. He babbled at the cereal right before reducing it to crumbs and tossing it onto the wooden floor like party confetti.

"Great," Trish said.

Randel chuckled. "Told you." He pulled away before heading to the refrigerator to retrieve a carton of eggs and butter. He set them on the counter. "I got a call from Ms. Carol on my business phone. I have no idea how she got my work number." He headed for the pan cupboard to grab a skillet, then placed it on the flat stovetop.

"Yeah? What did she say?" Trish asked, pulling a broom from the cleaning cupboard next to the microwave.

"Well, first, I asked her why she didn't call you. Then I remembered why."

Trish remembered too. The last time she had seen Ms. Carol, Randel had to stop Trish from ripping the woman's red locks out. *No one* called Darwin a *problem child*. It was absurd. He was a baby doing baby things. The other kid should've moved before the toy truck hit him in the face. That single action didn't deserve psychological observation. All he needed was a timeout.

"What did she want?" Trish asked.

"Darwin bit a little girl."

Okay… A cold sweat broke across her brow. "What did the little girl do to him?"

"Nothing, according to Ms. Carol. The little girl was sitting there, minding her own business, when Darwin strode over and bit her." Randel turned the knob, igniting the stovetop. After grabbing a butter knife from the drawer, he sliced a small square and let it drop into the pan.

"Well…" Trish shook her head. Doubt fogged her mind and penetrated her theory on Darwin just doing *baby things*. But the last thing she needed was for Randel to get upset and start worrying about their son. Who knew where his interrogation and overthinking could lead? "Well, it's probably a phase. You know how kids can be, right?"

Randel cracked an egg and dumped its guts into the pan. The smell of sulfur was strong, and nausea crept through Trish's gut. She held back a gag. *Dammit, I hate breakfast time,* she thought. It was almost as bad as Randel's garlicky and onion-based dinners. But those types of dinners were few and far between. Breakfast always stunk unless it was cereal and cereal only.

"He bit her on the neck, Trish. I mean, if it were her arm, or even her damn forehead, I'd say, yeah, okay, whatever. I mean, still weird…but whatever. But he bit her neck."

"He's teething." Her mouth moistened as the putrid smell intensified. She didn't understand how humans ate stuff like garlic, onions, or eggs. The sulfur was assaulting to the senses, making her eyes water. She avoided eating them altogether. They burned her esophagus and tore into her gut. She'd experienced it once, and that was enough. It was baffling how the scent stung more now, after her pregnancy. During her pregnancy, Darwin loved food; he stopped it from making her sick.

"Yeah, that's true." Randel stepped over to the cupboard next to the fridge, pulled out a loaf of whole wheat bread, and set it next to the toaster. Then he pulled a plate down and placed it next to the loaf.

Trish leaned the broom against the counter before crossing her arms. "So, what does she think we should do? It's just a phase. She's a teacher, she should know that." Trish looked over at Darwin, who continued to transform his cereal into a mound of mess on the floor. She snatched the broom and started sweeping it up.

"She said something about reading a few books and getting a psychologist to monitor him."

Tsk. "Again with that mess? Look, there's nothing wrong with our kid, Randel. He'll grow out of biting other kids, just like he'll grow out of destroying the kitchen floor with any solid food we try to feed him. So, call her back, and tell her no." She looked at him. "Easy fix."

"I told her I'd talk to you before we reached a decision, because she's going to have to meet with you and—"

"Why?" Trish asked.

"I have to head to the airport in an hour. I won't be able to see her today or for the rest of this week. Boy, was she pissed when I told her that. She went on and on about how she called my phone many times, then she had to look me up in my company's directory," he said. "Woman's nuts…"

Trish stopped sweeping. "What do you mean?" she asked, narrowing her eyes as disappointment flared in her chest. She had to be sure she had heard him correctly, so she approached him. "You're going out of town?"

"Yeah, I—" Realization crossed his face and dragged his brow. "Oh no." He shook his head slowly. "Sweetie, I'm *so* sorry. I totally forgot that—"

"Come on, hun. You knew I had a trip to Indiana tonight."

"That's right, and I'm so sorry, Trish. I totally forgot. I have to go. You know how Zeeland Electronics is. I've been working on them for *two years* now and they finally called us last night asking to upgrade to our latest software package. I guess their accounting app crashed, and Gabe wants me over there right away. The commission on this one is *huge* and I—"

"You're going all the way to Denver?" She raised a brow.

He nodded. "Yeah, and I figured I stay with my parents while I was there too. They're getting up there—Tell you what, when I come back, I'll take you for a nice steak dinner. And then we can take the boat out. Do that thing we do when no one is looking." He winked.

The boat, *The Weston World,* was a family treasure. They'd taken it out on many family excursions; it was Randel's favorite bribing tool. He'd even taken clients out on it just for them to come back to shore as the best of friends. *Too bad Zeeland Electronics didn't get to take a ride,* she thought. Trish had taken it out to dump body parts and all sorts of evidence. But, just as many other things in her part of their lives, he didn't need to know that. Trish sighed. "Alright. I'll hold you to that."

"Anyway," he said, changing the subject back to the matter at hand. "I told Ms. Carol that she'd have to meet with you, and she got desperate. She said *we* had to meet about Darwin before he can go back to school. So, we are meeting with her tomorrow at three. You will go into the classroom, and I will be there, but on a Zoom call."

Silence.

"Hun, please don't be mad," he said.

"I thought you would be home to watch Darwin tonight. You know how much I was looking forward to seeing Hilary."

Trish had convinced Randel that Hilary was a real person, and *she* had been the perfect cover for years. He'd even bought her a Christmas card every year. Trish promised to mail them, but she dumped them in her storage unit—something else that he didn't need to know about.

"I know, and I got you covered. Just call Maggie." He turned his back to fluff his eggs.

Trish sighed, hating when he spoke with sarcasm underneath his tongue. "I don't—"

"I know, I know, I know. You're possessive of our kid, but you have to let him socialize more often. That's probably why he's so grumpy now. You coddle him too much."

Trish frowned. "How so?"

He faced her. "Uh, for starters, you have to let him go to day-care more than fifteen hours a week, Trish."

"Well, he can't talk. How will I know what's going on over there? I don't want him there at all, actually, but—"

"I'm happy I overruled you because that's ridiculous. Let him adjust to having a babysitter. Come on, the boy needs to be around other people."

"I—"

"If you don't want Maggie staying over too long, have your Wednesday night out here, in town. That way, you get to hang out *and* coddle Darwin all in one day. You deserve it."

Trish sighed. Sarcasm. But Randel had a point; she could cancel her trip out of town and take a yoga and movie night that'd turn into a bar-hopping night, all of which were fake plans and always ended with a dead person and her full belly.

But she only trusted Randel with their child, not Maggie— the pot-smoking college kid. Trish knew for certain the girl didn't smoke inside their home, but the skunky THC still burrowed its way through Maggie's two percent body fat. How the girl remained admitted in any college program was a mystery to Trish. Maggie didn't seem to have much ambition. Her lackadaisical attitude left little to the imagination. Trish pictured Maggie watching television and playing on her phone whenever she got Darwin down for bed, not studying or reading. Or at least she brought nothing over to their house other than her phone. Trish didn't recall ever seeing Maggie with a book or a laptop.

But Randel enjoyed having the girl around. She was nice and caring…or so he said.

Trish huffed. With Randel heading out of town, she had to call Maggie. Trish's stomach crawled at her newfound frustration. The night didn't feel ideal. But with her hunger pains, no one was safe: not her neighbors, and maybe not even Randel.

No. She had to go out that evening, but with limited time, she was left with poor pickings. Trish thought hard while gawking at her husband, silently hoping he'd reconsider his own plans.

His unmoved stare said otherwise. "I have to go to that meeting." He turned to the stove and removed his eggs from the hot pan. He turned the stove off, then looked at her. "Call Maggie."

Trish grunted, allowing defeat to fester. She didn't argue, especially with men, and especially over something so trivial. Trish swallowed her pride and racked her mind. She had to hunt close by and at a place she knew—a place with something *big* happening—a place she hadn't been in a while.

A place where missing people could go unnoticed for a few days.

"All right," she said aloud.

"Good. So, we got that handled. What about Darwin's biting situation? What should we do until the meeting? Maggie isn't open to watch him during—"

"He can stay here with me."

Randel raised a brow. "Really? Will you be able to get any work done? We could have Maggie take him out for a few hours. I don't think she has a class today."

"Yeah. Once I put him down for a nap, I'll hop ahead. This month is amazingly slow anyway." She walked over to Darwin. "He can stay with me."

Trish smiled and rubbed his hair. He threw his head back and grinned at her.

Her smile faded.

A sharp bone pierced Darwin's gum—top, front, and center.

CHAPTER 6

Thirty-Seven

Trish's fingers neglected to make words on the keyboard, declaring her efforts to remain sluggish for most of the workday. It wasn't like she didn't try. She'd gotten dressed, wearing jeans and a light pink blouse, and she prepared her desk with everything she needed to get things done: a red pen, a fully charged laptop, and a jug of water. She'd even had her phone on silent, making it impossible to obsess about the notifications that she'd set; namely, those having to do with missing persons cases or crime scenes that she had everything to do with. With everything set up for a productive workday at her home office, she still didn't have the will or focus to get things done.

Trish rolled her tongue, then let out a soft groan. It was a stupid exercise, pretending that she was distracted from work when it was the other way around. She needed work to distract her from the thoughts of her child biting another kid. To distract from the fact that she was starving, and that she didn't have the luxury of going to Indiana to visit one of the many dingy bars on the interstate to get her fill for the month. So she opted for petty tongue movements and rocking in her chair as she frolicked in the bedrock of menial distractions.

She blew strands of hair from her face, watching them sway away and fall back onto her nose. Some strands were silver, but most of them were raven. Sometimes—and only sometimes—it was entertaining to watch her human form age. She was sure that the ring made her body about thirty-seven years old. Small wrinkles formed around her thick lips and eyes, and there was a small beauty mark next to her right eye that got slightly bigger over time. Her breasts were sagging a little too. She never went to a doctor; she gave birth to Darwin in her tub with the help of her doula and current close friend, Pita, but the last time she had gotten her blood checked was by Albert in the 1920s. She closed her eyes, thinking of Albert's ashen face and whitening hair when he learned his wife was a monster. She shoved the memory of him back into the recesses of her old mind.

The ring was on its own timer, making her age slower than the normal human. She thought she was canine in her new nature, seeing that dogs aged in the same manner with one year equaling seven to eight human years, but dogs aged faster with their escalating years, whereas she aged much slower.

Ah, to be human, she mused.

Darwin lay belly-down in his playpen, his thumb in his mouth and butt in the air. He snored on his plush blanket. It was cute how the boy got tuckered out from chatting in his beginner's language. Her body went warm as she smiled at him, and she decided the moments with Darwin would be the closest she'd get to pure happiness *and* true dread. She was happy to have known him, but depressed to watch him wither away, just as her husbands had throughout her existence on a planet that she understood just as much as she understood her own anatomy.

Darwin would leave one day, just like everyone else.

Trish sighed and shifted her attention to the computer monitor. A few fragmented thoughts took up very little of the white screen:

The Super Soaker for every home, with nano technology that gets grime from—

The grime-killing technology that g—

I'm hungry...

The instruction manual wasn't coming together—she'd been stuck on it for a couple of days. Trish deleted the last line and minimized the document's screen. It wasn't due for another two weeks; there was still time.

She twisted in her computer chair but stiffened when a cramp shot up her side. The last fourteen days of the month had been the hardest since Darwin was born, forcing her hunger pains to show up sooner than the regular three months. That's the way it had always been. *Feed seasonally*, she had been told all those years ago—over an entire *century* ago. But now...now she had to feed before becoming ravenous. Her tongue tingled more readily at the sight of a human outside her house. The smell of anything that Randel cooked made her want to vomit, as if her body were upset about the very unwanted food in her vicinity.

Hunger pains ignited in her gut, making her buckle. Trish couldn't gather the focus she needed for her job or the focus she needed to care for Darwin. The thought of her failing as a mother and a wife made her tear up.

No. That could not be her life, starving and wavering. She swiped tears away. Her feeding schedule needed some serious tweaking. But how?

Take the trip, she thought. It killed her to call Maggie for such a reason, when Randel, Darwin's father, should've stayed home and missed *his* trip. Not Trish.

Maggie was a stranger, and she was too close to Trish's things when Trish wasn't around. And if Maggie were around at the wrong time, she could become a meal. And Trish got the impression that Maggie would rather be somewhere else, smoking weed or playing on her phone; she seemed so disconnected.

As Trish stood from her seat, she tussled with her thoughts and the pangs creeping through her gut. She huffed and threw her head back, glaring at the ceiling.

Darwin liked Maggie.

Darwin likes everyone except that kid he bit.

She wiped the tears clean from her face again, cursing her emotions for bringing back traits that died for a while—was that the 70s?—only to come back this time around.

Compassion and generosity and care and...

Blood. Blood, I need food.

"But where?" she asked herself aloud, pacing her way into the living room. She envisioned the city, Grand Rapids. It would be quick and easy to snatch someone up from there. She could stop at a bar, scoop someone up, take them to an alley and then boom, dump them in a dumpster. She'd pose as a prostitute or start a fake Tinder account. Done.

No, she thought. *Won't work.* She'd been there six months ago, and they were still looking for the girl's body. The local news mentioned her, Holly Nelson, at least once a day. There were pleas all over social media and posters all over the metro area. It was impossible not to see her olive-toned face, trusting smile, and starry green eyes. She was so naïve, following Trish away from the bar, away from her friends, all for a fling with a stranger in some car on some back road.

There were many theories about Holly's disappearance, but Trish put the rumors to rest in her own mind. The girl hadn't been raped, murdered, and buried in the boonies. The girl hadn't been sold into the sex trade. And no, she wasn't being held captive in some lonely man's basement.

The girl had been eaten, drained dry, and sat at the bottom of Grand River, which was miles outside of the city, far enough for her never to be found.

Trish shook her head. No, it was still too hot to go back to the city.

She thought about the nearby dives and the highways stretching across the state, headed every which way. Then she pouted, preferring to stake those places out from afar…noting the mood and culture. Times and shifts. Camera angles.

There simply wasn't time.

Trish smacked her lips, feeling a lump grow in her throat.

It's been over a century, and I still don't understand this shit.

Since Darwin, things had been…different, forcing her to feed more often, manifesting into a frequent need, no longer a seasonal one. But feeding so often wasn't ideal. There were only so many places in West Michigan: the city, small towns, the occasional village, dive bars and truck stops. She'd been to many of them, but not all.

Why though? The question was saddening, and her constant need to understand her own morphology was tiring.

But she needed to eat.

She closed her eyes. Her thoughts jumbled, throwing her mind into a whirlwind. Nothing plausible formed. She didn't have a plan. Only the word *blood* popped up.

Trish paused, getting nowhere. Instead, she got ready for an uncertain night.

She went into her office and checked on Darwin. He stretched his small limbs and turned on his side. Then he curled into a ball.

Careful to leave the door open behind her, she stepped out into the living room and ran down to their bedroom. Inside the closet, she scanned over her many options and Randel's too. He was the king organizer, arranging their clothes by style: business casual, dress clothes, suits, and then jeans. Her clothes hung on the far right, in order by season. It was imperative that the house stayed organized and clean, anything to facilitate Randel's neatness. Randel even mopped, vacuumed, and did laundry twice a week, making it exceptionally hard to hide things from him.

Trish had always done her own laundry from *yoga nights* by leaving them in the car until Randel was at the office. Then she'd bring them in and wash or burn them in the fire pit early enough in the day for him not to notice that the pit had been used. If he ever found out the true meaning of yoga night, he'd be devastated—and maybe even faint. So, she took extra care to check her full outfit, sleeve, collar, and all.

In the closet, she separated the section where her fall clothes hung, picked up her sports duffle bag, and tossed it on the bed.

That should've been a suitcase, she griped to herself, reminiscing over the trip to Indiana that wasn't happening. No need for the suitcase now.

Randel's dress shoe collection sat on the shelf. The different colors and textures, such as snakeskin and leather, gleamed in the yellow light. The attic door was just above the shelf—more like the door to the roof. They never used it for storage because no one was small enough to crawl into the space. Except Darwin—he'd probably sit there and pull insulation foam from the floor and ceiling and shove it into his mouth.

Trish went over to the oak dresser, opened the top drawer, and grabbed a pair of leggings and a baby-blue sleeveless shirt. She tossed them next to the bag. Then she grabbed another pair of balled-up socks and added them to the pile.

She headed for the hallway and took a washcloth from the linen closet along with one of the twenty or so beach towels, something Randel wouldn't notice missing. She was always careful in marriage because domestic partnerships were a must. They not only offered a strong alibi but also some sense of control, something she lacked in the beginning. Her own mother could attest to that; it's how Trish turned into the monster she had become.

She slowed down her pace and found herself dazed at the memory of the girl she once was. The young, carefree woman from another time. Sometimes she wished she could go back, and sometimes she did. In fact, she wasn't sure what people thought about when they drifted off to sleep. Well, she asked her husbands and very few friends just that, and their answers varied: *I think about what I have planned the next day*, or *I think about my kids*, or *I think about something I ate and how much I liked it or didn't like it*. But Trish thought about Momma's reddened face and angry shouting. She thought about the last night she saw her only family member.

PART 3

Sweet Home,
West Virginia

CHAPTER 7

1889

The sun had nearly fallen into the horizon when a crisp, chilly breeze weaved through Skinner's Gap as it crossed the Northern Appalachian Mountains. It was refreshing on Trish's sweaty face as she dragged a stack of woven baskets up the rocky trail as she approached home. The top basket, full of apples and pears, wore on her young arms and her high-top leather shoes dug into the backs of her feet. Her burgundy, full length calico dress collar was wet with sweat, the bottom of it dragged on the dusty ground. But finally, the flickering lantern lights outed the wooden porch, which had been scorched by the winter chill and burned by the summer sun.

Momma marched out of the cabin with a broom in hand, its angry unkempt brush and splintering handle having seen better days. She used her big hands to sweep up nothing; she only moved dust around, forming a beige cloud that encased her thick shins, and the willow rocking chair that spent most of its best days in the shade. Her dark hair was pulled back, and her once white apron looked stained orange, her plaid dress underneath it may have suffered the same fate. Trish was sure Momma slaughtered the swine Josef brought over a couple days before, or it could've been an unlucky hen. There was no telling. Trish only knew it was food because something smelled good and she was hungry.

Momma leaned the broom against the doorframe and picked up the rocking chair with one hand to pull it inside. "Patricia," she shouted. "Where's Josef at? Why are you luggin' that shit 'round?"

"Ugh," Trish said. Why did it matter? "Josef is where he's at," she said, annoyed at Momma's constant inquiries about Josef as if he were their personal savior.

"Fine. Make things harder on yourself din'. When you done unloadin' that stuff, go 'round back, clean the coop, and lock up. Suppa'll be ready in 'bout an hour."

Trish stopped and slouched; her sore arms and legs stiffened. "I'm tired, Momma," she grumbled.

"Don't start with me, Patricia. It ain't my fault that you won't let dat boy help ya out. That's what he's for, right?"

No, Trish thought. She knew how some men were, especially when they were a certain age. They'd start with helping with chores and telling the girl how pretty she was. Next thing the girl knows, she's standing in the kitchen barefoot with three kids hanging from her apron and one balled up in her belly. That wasn't for Trish. She ran away from that life like Josef ran away from the mines.

"Fine," Trish said, too exhausted to voice her grievances to Momma. She dragged her feet along the dusty, gravelly path that led up to the cabin. She dropped the baskets at the foot of the porch steps and made her way around back. She watched the deep orange horizon fade, and the sky turn night blue and evening purple. Silver dots were unveiled in the east, offering light that didn't set with the sun. The mountain range rested in its own shadow as day turned into night. It would go on to be a sight Trish would never forget: the Appalachian sunset.

"Hey, Patricia!" A familiar voice from behind.

She spun around to find Josef approaching, Misty pulling his cart up the dirt road. Josef sat on an empty cart, having sold all his family's wool. Trish didn't find Josef attractive. His blond mop was always sticky with sweat, and his fair skin was riddled with black-heads and gray blemishes. Josef Beck, and the rest of the Beck family, didn't believe in baths. And though he smelled like a pigsty, Trish found him pleasantly entertaining, especially when he got drunk, and even more when he got *her* drunk. They only laughed and talked bad about everyone in town: her favorite type of entertainment.

"Why'd you leave? I looked all ova' for ya." Josef pouted.

"I was tired," she said as she walked up to Misty. She rubbed the mule's black mane. Misty pulled away and sighed in response. Trish smiled, wishing she had a mule or horse. She'd brush it and talk to it. Treat it like more than just a tool to haul harvest and meat around.

"You know I would'a brought ya here." Josef frowned, displeased.

"It's all right, *Josef*," she teased. His cheeks blushed. "I saw you down there talkin' to your pa. I didn't wanna interrupt."

Josef dropped his head, tilting his hat. "He wants me t'go work down at the mines."

"Good. You'll make more money."

"Yeah, dat's what he said. But I like bein' a farmhand. I git to talk to people in town. I git to sell my own stuff—" He smiled. "I git to hang out every night."

Trish wished she could work in the mines. She'd bring in more money—save enough to do whatever she wanted. And it would be a good excuse to avoid everyone in town. Time away from Momma wouldn't hurt either. But they didn't hire women for those types of jobs. She was doomed to be a farmhand. "I wish we could switch places."

"Then you wouldn't have time to hang out wit me."

"You mean so I can listen to your daily drunken rants? What was it last night? Uh…Oh. Oh," she said, chuckling. "Remember last night when you were all, *'Oh, if Pa wants that shit sold, he'll get his fat ass down there and do it hisself.'* You were drunker than shit complainin' about how much you hated this stuff, and now you gotta chance to get out of it—a chance to make more money—and you don't wanna do it. You funny."

They laughed.

"Heck yeah. Anyways," he said, flagrantly skirting the subject as he often had. "How'd you do in town today? I sold the last of the wool." He looked over at her stack of baskets near the porch. "Looks like you did good too."

"What's dis? A competition?" she asked.

"No. I'm jus' sayin'. A pretty girl like you shouldn't have trouble sellin' crop."

"And I neva' do."

"Yeah, I know. Did ya' momma get the wool today? Pa said he was goin' to bring it right over dis mornin' in exchange for some eggs."

She shrugged. "I jus' got here." She sighed and kicked at the dirt, getting it on Misty's legs. Trish waited for a reaction, but the animal didn't seem to notice; she went on chewing whatever was in her mouth, which could have been air for all Trish knew.

"You a'ight?"

"No. How fair do dis sound: I've been sittin' up at the market all day sellin' our stuff while she's been doin' nothin'. And now she wants me to clean out the coop before I lock up."

Josef threw his head back and chuckled. His gullet jumped with amusement as his blond chin stubble glistened in the setting sun. "You terrible," he said.

"I'm tired," she said again, dropping her shoulders.

"Sure, sure. Don't do dat very *simple* task."

She shrugged. "I oughta come out here and do it later."

Josef's smile quickly faded into a frown. "Y-you're going to come out here at-at night? Alone?" He leaned in. "You ain't scared?"

She took a step back. "Scared of *what*?"

"The beast. That's all they keep talkin' about. Somethin's goin' 'round snatchin' up stock."

Trish shook her head. "Dat's uh myth!" She giggled. But when he only frowned, she went on. "It's just a mountain lion gettin' ready for winter. Happens every year."

"Nah. No mountain lion takin' out a whole herd unda' eight hours."

"Who said? Cutler?"

"Well...yeah."

"Really? Oh-oh, lemme guess...you guys were drinkin'?"

"Yeah—we– That ain't the point. The point is—"

"My *God*, Josef, Cutler is a bumblin' drunk. He probably din killed his own flock while he was floatin' aroun' in a blackout. He probably knocked them all out with his stankin' ass whiskey breath. I swear the man's blood *is* alcohol. He doesn't have to worry 'bout anything attackin' him unless it wants to be drunk off its ass."

Josef didn't laugh that time either. "Cutler was pretty shuck up. Said he found a bloody pasture wit' bits of muscle and an ear here and a detached hoof there. He was pretty sure his farm was attacked as he slep'."

"Sure, sure. You're worried 'bout me, but you're the one who needs to watch who you believe, Josef." She raised her brow.

Josef looked off into the distance as night ate the sky, feeding the growing blackness to the hill's shadows. "Well, I'll be out for a while. I'm actually heading over Cutler's now. You want some help? Get it all done now and come out for a few drinks with us?"

Trish pursed her lips. Although she was looking forward to having some drinks, Josef's whining about getting a better job and concern over the fabled beast made her want to vomit. And spending the evening with Cutler? *No thank you.* "Nah," she said. "I'm tired. Have fun though."

"Alright. Watch yourself out here. I hope you change your mind and just wait 'til mornin'."

"Are you insane? Momma wouldn't let me hear the end of it. I'll take my chances. Stop by in a couple days. I might need a drink." Trish winked at him.

He blushed. "Promise me you watch yourself out here, pretty lady."

She raised her right hand. "I promise. But, uh, worry 'bout yourself. You're the one walkin' 'round the woods at sundown."

"Don't worry 'bout me. I got ol' Misty and my gun here." Josef leaned forward and patted Misty's rump. Then he reached over to the passenger seat of the cart and patted the shotgun that Trish carried when she rode along with him. Most people carried their gun around at night to fend off animals, and if they headed down to Virginia. Road bandits were a major presence back then.

"I'll see you in a couple days," Josef said before winking and smiling as he prompted Misty to turn and head back on the trail leading to the main road.

Trish nodded. "Good night."

She headed back for the chicken coop and saw the gate wide open. She grumbled. "I guess it's alright for *you* to leave the gate open. But when I do it, all hell breaks loose. Forget it." Trish grabbed the fence and slammed it shut. "They should have enough feed to get them through the night," she said, justifying her lethargy. She picked up the rope that had been left in the gravel and wrapped it around the fence, pinning it shut.

***

Trish found Momma filling porcelain bowls with pork and potato soup. It smelled savory and fresh, making her mouth water. Trish headed over to the pot of warm water that sat on the counter next to the iron stove and dipped her hands inside. She rubbed them together, cleaning off the dirt.

"Saw Josef out there," Momma said as she set the bowls on the table, one on either end.

"I saw 'em too," Trish said as she shook her hands dry and headed for her seat.

Momma handed Trish a hand towel and smiled. "Alright. And..."

Trish sat in her favorite wooden chair, back to the door, front facing the kitchen. She reached for her spoon as Momma sat across the wooden table, facing the door and Trish. "*And* nothing. He's just anotha kid das dragged into doing stuff he don't wanna do."

"Oh, trust me, Patricia, be lucky that dat's all ya'll gotta do. Live worry-free while you can, because it ain't gettin' easier."

"I'mma make it easier," Trish mumbled as she went to take a bite. She blew on the brewing soup first.

"Sure you will. You have the answers to everythin'. Maybe you can figure out a safe way to slay the beast. I know you heard 'bout it. Dats all the town's been talkin' about." Momma ate a spoon full.

This again? Trish thought. She looked up at Momma and grinned. "I already figured out how to kill it."

Momma set her spoon down and looked at Trish intensely. "Mind sharin' your plans?"

"Yup. I'll jus' talk it to death."

To Trish's surprise, Momma laughed. Trish chuckled but decided to dive into a conversation before Momma decided the remark wasn't funny anymore. She cleared her throat. "What do you think they'll do once they find it? The imaginary beast?"

"Kill it and use it. Lord knows there are people in town who need meat and fur for winter."

Trish nodded in agreement, even though she was sure people would die that winter anyway, just as they died every winter. She and Momma were lucky. Although they worked overtime to keep a living, it *was* a living. They never went hungry or cold, and Trish intended to keep it that way with or without Momma's help.

"Thanks for cleanin' out the coop," Momma said as she wiped her lips with a napkin and placed it back on the table. "My back been stiff and hurtin' bad lately; it woulda put me down for a week if I fooled around with them damn birds. You know how they get; they won't eat if their coop dirty."

"Well, I closed it. I ain't cleaned it."

Momma's face dropped into a scowl as she placed her full spoon back into her bowl. "Why not?"

"Because I'm tired. I can do it in the mornin'."

"That's not what I told you to do!" Momma shouted.

With no chance of reneging the truth, Trish decided to stand her ground. "It ain't a big deal. I can do it at sunup."

"But I told you to do it before supper! You don't listen to anythin' I say!"

"Momma, calm down, it's not that—"

"Don't tell me to calm down, damnit! You laze 'round, give me attitude when I ask you to do somethin', and then you blow it off as if anythin' I ask you to do mean nothin'! I'm sick of it!"

Trish raised her voice. "It's fine! It's ain't like they're going to die if they sleep in a dirty coop. It ain't the end of the world! I don't understand why you so upset!"

Momma closed her eyes and pinched the bridge of her nose. She sighed, then calmly said, "You know what? Don't worry about it. I'll do it because you can't be botha'ed. You so damn *lazy*, and I don't know who you got it from. It wasn't me! And it definitely wasn't yo' father."

Trish's nose flared at the mere mention of him. She hadn't met the man, and didn't know him from Adam. How dare Momma bring that up as if it mattered? As if he ever been present? "How do you know? He died before the real work started. It's like one day he was like, *Oh, we pregnant? Oh, you gotta farm in the mountains? Oh nice, let me get drunk and jump off the nearest cliff.*"

Momma sprung up from her seat, rounded the table, and slammed her open palm onto Trish's cheek. Her thick palm shoved flashes before Trish's eyes.

Trish held her face and looked at Momma, stunned. Momma had never moved that fast before. The ordeal gave Trish whiplash.

"Don't *ever* say that about him," Momma said, her voice shaky. "He died on accident, and for you to even consider any other cause, 'specially suicide, brings me *deep* shame."

"How could you hit me over that? He left us!" Trish sobbed and held onto her stinging cheek. "I hate you," she shrieked.

"Then gone an' get married! You nineteen! You can go start a life of yo' own! You don't need ta' stay unda' me! Be my guest, darlin' girl!" Momma huffed, her nostrils spreading wide as angry air shot from her reddening face and onto Trish's forehead. Trish dared not say a word as Momma continued. "But if you *gotta* stay here cuz you refuse to find a nice man to start a life wit, so be it. You are my daughter, and I love you mo' than anythin' in this world. I will *neva* turn on you. But as long as you livin' on this farm—the farm where I alone raised you—the farm that take care of us—the farm that helped you grow up…you *will* live by my rules. You understan'?"

Trish didn't respond. Not only did her face hurt—she flicked her teeth with her tongue to make sure none were knocked loose— she was overcome by Momma's face. Momma's tight lips quavered and her eyes watered; her disappointment was too much to bear. Trish glared down at the table, falsely focusing on the tabletop underneath her supper, which was getting cold. Still, she searched for a hurtful retort—hurt Momma more than she hurt Trish. Maybe it would relieve some of the sorrow she felt. But the words didn't come. Only silence.

"Don't worry 'bout the coop," Momma said as she turned and headed for the other side of the table. "I'll clean it in the mornin'. Go to your room. I can't look at you right now."

Trish slammed her palms onto the tabletop and rose quickly. The right thing to do was to go off to her room and leave everything as it was. She didn't like hurting Momma that bad. She liked it when Momma laughed at her wise-ass banter. It made Trish feel more like an adult…no longer Momma's kid, but her best friend. She didn't mean for Momma to get so upset. It almost killed her to see Momma's face wet with tears and voice shaken with hurt. But instead of apologizing, Trish stood her weakening ground. "I don't understan' why you so upset over somethin' so stupid! It ain't a big deal. I'll just go and clean the damn thing right now!" Trish headed for the door.

"No! You are not leavin' this house!"

"Why? It wasn't a problem a month ago. A year ago. I been goin' out at night fa' years. What's so different now?"

"Patricia, no! You will not be leavin' this house—don't you dare leave this house until sunup!" Momma shook like a leaf as she cried and raced for Trish.

"Mo—"

"Patricia, just go to yo' room! I'll clean it!"

Trish narrowed her eyes at Momma. "I cleaned the coop at night all da time. What's the problem now? Why can't I—"

"I don't want you outside at night."

"I—" Trish started until something dawned on her. "You…you think the beast is real? You-it… It's just a—" She sighed. Then she giggled. It all made sense. Cutler's asinine story scared Momma. Trish softened her voice. "Look, I can do it. I can go clean it and nobody gotta go to bed mad. I can jus' go do it—"

"I'll be happy when you go to yo' room. For once, listen to what *I say*. Now!"

Momma's words pierced Trish's soul, chilling her inside because she was worried about nothing, and it was saddening.

Trish dragged her feet back to her room and closed the door behind her. She didn't bother slamming it, because she was still in awe. Momma was the strongest person Trish knew. But her fear was unfounded. Josef, Cutler, and the whole town was on edge about a beast that nobody saw.

"It's a damn mountain lion," Trish growled. Then she imagined a mountain lion feasting on Cutler's goats and laughed.

CHAPTER 8

Grown Up

Trish lay on her bed fully dressed, having not moved from her spot since Momma banished her to her room. She was sure Momma had gone to bed, because the angry clattering of dishes had stopped.

Trish sprung up and looked out the window. She was sure it was after midnight as the twilight dazzled and the round, white moon set high in the pitch-black sky. She headed for her room door and opened it slowly, hoping to diminish the earsplitting creaks of her temporary escape. Mastering the compression of the shrieking hinges had become an art for Trish, as she snuck out often.

This time would be no different.

Trish smiled, ready to show Momma that there was nothing wrong with cleaning the coop at night—she had done it many times before. Ol' drunk Cutler was full of shit and liquor. There was no wild beast lurking around in the shadows, taking out animals; there was only a family of hungry mountain lions getting ready for winter. Everyone in Hopkins, including Momma, had their encounters with the feral cats of the hills. It was normal. Every year, the men would go out, hunt down the alpha, and scare the rest of them back into the mountains. Cutler's slurred cries were only rumors made to scare people.

Damn fear monger, Trish thought as she grabbed a long stick from behind her door. The thin tree branch had been sharpened at the edge and stood half her size. She'd never leave the house at night without it. Although there was no beast, she would still shove her stake into the eye of a mountain lion, just like anyone else would. Just like anyone *always* had.

After leaving her room, she gently closed the door behind her. Trish tiptoed through the kitchen and stopped. She glared at the closed door next to the counter, which hid Momma's snoring form as she rested. Trish hoped Momma slept well in there, not worrying about her hardheaded daughter.

"I'm sorry," Trish whispered. Then she smiled, knowing how she'd make it all up. Momma would wake up to a clean coop and fresh scrambled eggs with oatmeal. She'd love breakfast, but she'd love Trish's news even more: Trish was going to get serious with Josef and build her own cabin. Maybe even buy Momma's massive front yard—build there. Trish even wanted Momma to know about her clothing business idea and how Trish was going to pay someone to help Momma around the farm. She'd ruminated long and hard as she lay in her bed, guilt encompassing her thoughts. She'd make everything right with Momma, and there was the best place to start.

Trish's heart lurched, excited about her new goals, and anxious not to wake Momma.

Walking on her toes, Trish crept past Momma's room and then across the living room. She kicked the rocking chair and listened to it creak as it rocked angrily. She froze and stared at Momma's room door with wide eyes. She listened, not hearing anything but snoring. Momma didn't toss or turn. She only slept.

She relaxed and picked up the lantern from the small table next to the door and silently thanked herself for filling it with gas the day before. She took a deep breath, put her stick underneath her armpit, and clutched the lantern handle in her hand. Then she opened the door slowly, allowing its strident groan to cut through the house. It was the loudest sound she'd ever heard. She peered at Momma's door, ready for her to charge out her room with the shotgun.

But there was nothing. No new urgent groans from the house, and no scuttling in Momma's room. Only snoring.

Trish stepped out into the cold night. Frosty wind nipped at her nose and ears as she closed the door and crossed her arms, retaining whatever heat she could hold while hugging her stick.

Should grab a coat, she thought. But it was too late to go back; it was much too risky. Instead, she walked across the grass, careful to avoid the pile of leaves Momma left in the middle of the yard when she'd raked earlier. Trish groaned. "But I'm lazy… Right."

Trish rounded the cabin, noting the aroma of burning leaves and wood, which gave her another idea. To further make up for her indiscretions, she would rake the yard and burn the leaves after breakfast. She was ready to show Momma that she didn't need to be told to take care of anything. Trish wasn't lazy, and she wasn't a kid anymore. She was a grown woman who would own part of the farm and build her and Josef's cabin a few feet away from Momma's. Making up her mind that that was the way things were going to go, she tossed a look over her shoulder and smiled at the forested part of the farm where there were too many trees for her or Momma to do anything with the land. She and Josef would do the work of clearing it out, no matter how long it took. They'd get out there at night once he got off work at the mines, working alongside singing cicadas in the roasting humid summers, and fending off frost-bitten fingertips in the bitter, freezing winter. Clearing the land alongside him would make her so tough that she'd feed her newborn baby and fight off a lion at the same time. She'd make clothes and dinner all at once.

She hummed as she basked in her planned accomplishments and the life she couldn't wait to get started on.

They'll agree, Trish thought. *They—*

All thoughts diminished as she drew closer to the coop. She heard nothing but night sounds and whipping crisp air. A thick shadow cloaked the outside of the coop that housed the oddly quiet hens.

Then she stopped, convinced her eyes were telling the truth as they uncovered what the night tried to hide.

There was no clucking or chicken chatter, and the pale white gate was open.

CHAPTER 9

The Coop

Trish watched the blackened entrance as her heart slammed into her chest. Chills ran down her back.

I closed the gate, she thought.

She aimed the sharp tip of her spear at the dark opening with one hand and raised her lantern with the other. She stepped slowly into the bleakness. The coop didn't seem familiar. Its shadowy aura had become part of the night. No amount of light seemed to show enough.

And the hens…they weren't bickering or chattering.

Trish tried to breathe normally, but fear choked her, forcing her breath to stagger. *Maybe Momma opened it?* she reasoned.

She shook her head, knowing better: Momma never left the gate open at night.

Maybe I forgot to close the gate…?

Trish searched her memory, struggling to find herself *locking the gate*. She remembered grabbing hemp rope off the ground. The prickly rope snagged her fingers as she tied it all while complaining about Momma.

Trish walked down the wooden ramp. Each step squeaked as she made her slow incline. Shaky lantern light exposed a small distance, but her hitched breath frothed into icy clouds, making it hard to see.

As she drew closer, she still couldn't hear birds. She heard *slurping*. She held her breath, perplexed by the unnatural sound. Wet and smacking lips sucked and bit and spit. Something was gorging on her flock. And it wasn't a mountain lion.

Icy blood coursed through her body as she shook violently while her orange flame uncovered the gory sight.

The figure sat on its haunches with its back to Trish. Charred flesh took up the spaces between islands of red and pink boils. Patches of dark hair clung to its leathery skull. The thing stopped sucking and biting a brown hen and spit out a mouth full of feathers.

Bloodied beaks, tattered pink meat, and ripped wattles littered the nests along the walls. And the feathers were everywhere. A lot of them lingered in the air alongside dust. The metallic air was wet with blood.

Trish gasped and went to back away on locked knees, but the creature stopped and turned, finding her. It tilted its head and glared at her with wide, pink eyes.

It unclasped its hands, allowing the carcass to slide from its lengthy bony fingers. It stood on thin legs, exposing its frame. He wasn't wearing clothes. Large burns reduced its limbs, sunken face, and flattened middle to a blistered mess. Its widened eyes floated, blazing as hard as a foreign star in the dead of night. It curved its thick wet lips into a smile showing blood-stained sharp teeth, happy to see her.

"You..." it hissed, a hint of elation on its tongue.

Cold wrapped her body tight, shaking her at the knees as the human-like creature spewed bloody words that filled the space between them. Dazed and going light on her feet, she was too terrified to faint.

"Yes, I've been looking for someone like you," it rasped. It inhaled deep and exhaled woefully.

Before she could question the beast, it darted and reached for her collar.

She dropped the lantern and spear as it snatched her off her feet. Trish's head thrashed and her neck stiffened. The beast plunged its pointy fingers into her shoulders as it slammed her onto the floor with brazen strength. Trish yelped as pain bolted up her back. As she kicked up dust, the light grew dark. Claws dug deep into her flesh as it moved his hands down to her arms. Trish shook and kicked, trying to break the beast's grip.

It sat across her lap, its bony buttocks digging into her pelvis. Her body strained, fighting for freedom. It grappled her with its knees, pinning her arms and hands to her sides.

"Help me!" she shrieked. "Momma! Momm—"

"Shhhh." A shaken hush escaped the monster's bloody mouth as it covered hers, slicing her cheeks as it gripped her face. Blood leaked from the new cuts and collected in her ears.

Sobbing and flailing, she watched as its pink eyes watched her back. They were enticed, longing, determined...*hungry.*

"Momma!" A muffled cry that stopped underneath the creature's rough hand as it leaned into her. It smelled like burning meat and hot iron.

It sniffed her right ear before shoving its slimy tongue inside. It groaned and hummed, deafening her. Then it moved its warm tongue down her face and stopped at her neck. The monster rubbed sharp teeth against her, pushing hard against her soft flesh.

Fangs punctured her neck, and she struggled to breathe through the onslaught of pain as achy waves coerced her shocked nerves. She went to scream again, but her tongue swelled, and her cries were silenced in her numb throat. The beast slurred and licked, feasting on her new wound. Trish's shoulders slacked as her arms became useless. Her body refused her thoughts; she was sedated. Everything eased into blackness as she listened to the creature's perpetual smacking and slurping. Her own blood was warm against her chilling skin.

Hazy and tired, Trish stopped moving. Her legs turned into heavy lumps as she closed her eyes. Her body floated on air as the pain subsided, leaving her to her last thoughts.

She'd never see Momma or Josef or anyone again. But they'd see her.

Dead, she thought. *Momma,* she thought, *I'm sorry.*

She couldn't feel teeth anymore. But she heard swallowing, and she smelled dead animals and metal.

Then she heard the call, a sound she hadn't heard around her house at night. An urgent sound. A welcoming sound that was getting close. *Dogs,* she thought. *Barking,* she reminded herself as the sound of angry hounds erupted in the short distance.

The beast pulled away from her neck quickly, warm spatter wetting the side of her face and chin. Then the albatross on her body had lifted.

Feet stomped across the wooden panels, taking the smell of death with it.

Bloodhounds barked and shrieked as they crushed leaves; shouting men accompanied them. They were all on her property.

Her head pounded and her heart slammed into her chest. She could've been laying in an ice bath as bitter chills shot though her limbs. Pain crept back into her bones and encompassed her neck and face. She cried as she slowly twisted at the waist, her muscles screaming in response.

The men grew closer, maybe a few feet away from the coop. Their demands for death rang deep in her ears. The ground seemed to shake with anger as rowdy voices penetrated the air.

Move, she thought. But she only lay there. Her limbs jerked and her eyes blinked hard. She swallowed, tasting blood. Her mind struggled to form thoughts as the wooden ceiling spun in the dark, tossing her into a mental whirlwind.

The coldness against her skin disappeared, and she felt numb to the chill. Tears formed as she cried.

Call for help, she thought.

Don't be stupid, she quickly rebutted.

All thoughts seized when a horrific spasm tore through her mouth, forcing her to her side. Her gums burned, then throbbed. She held her hand against her mouth, holding onto the pain and holding back the screams. Her muscles locked and let go, stealing her movements. She ran her tongue along her teeth. Two of them stuck out like knives. Her mouth filled with blood, with her tongue soaking first.

As the barking exploded in her ears and the foul smell of dog's breath encased her air, she closed her eyes. The *beast* had gotten her.

Cutler was right, she thought. She secretly apologized and searched for his voice amongst the crowd.

"Get em', boy!" one man said.

"I saw it run dis way!" another said.

A whimper escaped from her sore throat. Her face was still struck with aches as she swallowed her own blood.

She looked around, lifting her chin as far as she could. She saw nothing, but she could smell everything. The dead hens lay around in pieces and their blood painted the air while the rancid-mouthed dogs were right outside.

Cause of death: mistaken identity, she thought. She wished she could laugh at that, but she was too tired.

She shut her eyes and held her breath, ready for teeth to tear her flesh open. Ready for bullets to rip her body to bits. Ready for Momma to be awakened by all the barking and shouting and death.

But the barking and shouting slowly drifted away as the mob passed by. Trish allowed herself a rattled sigh. She rocked a little, hoping to lull the infuriated pangs down to minor aches. It only helped her move the pain around. She was careful not to use her tongue to check on her teeth; her gums were too tender and bled intensely.

She spit out more blood and felt the pain ease in her limbs, allowing her to get up. Or so she thought. But she decided to lie there and listen to the mob move off her property and back into the woods.

She smiled, then chuckled a bloody laugh. Her brief joy rewarded her with a new pain that gripped her lungs. She coughed to clear her throat, then she listened.

The shouting dogs weren't at all interested in chicken blood; they wanted the very *real* fabled beast. They wanted the monster who had been terrorizing her side of the mountain for a few weeks. They wanted the creature that had just attacked her.

CHAPTER 10

Friends and Neighbors

Trish stood in her office doorway, watching Darwin. He was asleep, snoring through his opened mouth. She watched the drool spill onto his blanket, and she chuckled. Whenever she put a blanket over him, he'd kick it off in a huff. But whenever she put him on top of the blanket, he'd fall right to sleep. He snored lightly and calmly, a resting angel.

But she wasn't watching his sleeping form. She was looking at his gums. The tooth hadn't broken through fully. It taunted her as it appeared to be growing sideways. The sharp edge of the ashen bone lying underneath a thin, gummy layer broke through enough to be seen.

Ugh, Trish thought, ready to wash her hands of the whole ordeal just as she had done with most things that came with her human persona. She didn't care about getting oil changes on time, being late on a timeline, or buying Chinese food instead of making dinner like she'd promised. But this wasn't going away. Everything from where Darwin bit the kid to how this tooth was growing bothered her. *And in the top gum too?* Her research told her kids grew their two front bottom teeth by the time they turned one. Not Darwin.

You're normal. You have to be normal. Kids bite people sometimes, she assured herself. Darwin did baby things. He acted out when he was up past his bedtime and cried when he didn't want to share his toys with Pita's kids. He whined when Trish or Randel dropped him off at daycare. He made messes. Laughed. Cried. Played. Her Darwin was *all* human. Thanks to the ring and thanks to his father.

There was nothing to prove.

Are you sure? she asked herself.

She shook her head, knowing that she wasn't sure and that the nagging doubt in the back of her mind wouldn't go away that easy. So, she did the next best thing: she picked up her phone and texted someone who'd agree with her.

Pita, a short, thin woman with tanned skin and dark hair, was Trish's personal baby guru. Not only did she serve as Trish's doula, Pita also had children, a two-year-old named Brady and a seven-year-old named Katie. Trish leaned on Pita's expertise most days, texting her about anything ranging from weird-looking rashes to different types of poops. Getting through Darwin's first year would've been impossible if not for her. Not only that, but Pita was also great at keeping a secret, having not told anyone about Trish's pregnancy. Even when Pita pressed Trish about Darwin's birth certificate, she assured her that she would take him to the hospital and get it all squared away. Trish had never done any of those things, having made all her identity paperwork and her son's birth certificate herself.

Still Pita kept her secret and never asked about it. Instead, she invited Trish out to coffee, water for Trish, and they'd talk and talk. Pita talked about her kids and family and Trish talked about the cute things Darwin had done that week. Their meetings left Trish understanding and knowing everything about Pita. Pita was one of the few people that Trish trusted with Darwin, more than she trusted Randel's parents, who only came in from Denver once a year. But sadly, Pita was just as busy as Trish. She had overseen many births in the last couple years after she left her nursing job at the hospital, leaving Trish to depend on the daycare and Maggie.

Still, Pita was more than a cloaking device, she was a decent friend. Trish pictured herself growing old with Pita, meeting up for yoga or coffee, water for Trish. They'd talk about their growing and grown-up kids, then talk about how Trish never seemed to age. To that, Trish chuckled, already having come up with a fake charcoal, age-defying face mask that only seemed to work for her. "It keeps me looking young," she planned on saying. Granted, Trish would move on from Pita once she died, but Trish vowed to never entangle Pita within her wrath, no matter what happened. Trish killed husbands and best friends, like Johnny and Mel. She didn't feel too bad about what happened to Johnny. She cared so little that she pushed his name from her thoughts. But Mel. The thought of Mel almost brought tears to Trish's eyes.

But Pita was not Mel. And Mel was not Pita. In fact, Mel no longer existed in anyone's world anymore.

With that, Trish texted: *Hey, you. How's your day going?*

The phone rang in response. Trish didn't mind the call. She kind of looked forward to Pita's venting about her afternoon drive from work or her drive to get Katie from school. It was *the* daily rant.

"How's it going?" Pita asked. Trish heard the wind blowing into the receiver. She pictured her friend pulling on a cigarette with the window cracked—all in pure Pita-like fashion. It was funny sometimes: a well-respected nurse sucking down cigarette smoke. It was poison; Trish could smell the nicotine and arsenic from a mile away.

"I could be doing better. Hey, I have a question to ask you, if that's all right."

"Shoot."

Trish paused before her office window. The house across the street, a brick tri-level a lot like hers, had finally gotten new occupants. A tall man wearing gray joggers and a white t-shirt unloaded a silver minivan that was parked in the driveway. He hefted a box up to his broad chest and crossed the yard to the walkway that led up to the house. His bare mahogany dome glinted in the high sun. He headed for a short woman with wide hips who stood in the doorway with her arms out, ready to receive the box. Her hair was short and curly, and her mocha skin was deep and rich, much like the models that Trish had seen on those facial cleanser commercials. She, too, was dressed down, with leggings and a pink blouse. They moved casually, in no big rush.

"Darwin's been biting kids at school. Is that normal?" Trish said softly. She held her breath, half-expecting a sputter of disbelief from her friend.

"Fuck *yeah* that's normal. Katie nearly bit her own damn fingers off when she was teething, and Brady bit a kid in the head because he wouldn't share blocks."

"Mmm." Trish watched the man outside carry a box the size of a forty-two-inch TV. He handed it to the woman, who took it inside. "That's bizarre."

"I know, right? I told you, kids are something *else*. I wouldn't worry about it."

Would you worry if your baby's teeth grew in sharp?

"Okay. That's great. So, there's nothing to worry about then," Trish said. "The teacher wants to meet with Randel and me before Darwin can go back. I think it's a little dramatic."

"Seriously?" Trish pictured Pita scrunching her face. "*Ugh*. Some teachers just don't feel like dealing with that *one* kid that's a teeny bit different from their peers. Anyway, he's fine."

"Yeah, I'm sure you're right."

The man outside dropped a vase. An earsplitting shatter cut through the quiet. His shoulders raised a little, and his mouth dropped. Slowly, he looked at the doorway, where the woman had returned.

The woman exclaimed something as she strutted over.

"I know. I always am." Pita chuckled. "Anyway, still up for brunch next week, right? I have to fill you in on this wedding mess. My brother's bride is *trite*. It took everything out of me not to strangle her the other day. Trish, let me tell you, planning is *not* her strong suit. I feel like I should have done the whole thing on my own!"

"Yeah? How is that?" Trish watched the man scramble to pick up the shards while his wife crouched and snatched up fragments alongside him, yelling and aggravated.

"Well," Pita said, "she wants her colors to be this dirty-looking gray and sherbet pink and… Oh girl, I have to tell you all about it."

The woman outside rose quickly from the ground, standing straight on her short haunches. She squinted hard, and a pained look crossed her face. She cradled her hand, and blood crawled down her pink sleeve, soaking it in red.

Trish's body ached, and her stomach grumbled. "I can't wait to hear all about it," she said, her tongue watering, imagining the savory taste in her mouth.

"Okay. I gotta go. I'm picking Katie up from school."

"Okay, bye." Trish hung up before Pita could say anything else. *Time to meet the neighbors*, she thought.

She rushed into the kitchen, where she snatched a few paper towels free from the roll. Then she hurried through the house, eager to bask in the savory tease before the night ahead.

Before—many decades ago—Trish couldn't get close to humans if she was hungry. Reckless and young, she had taken advantage of the times where the police were inept to mysterious happenings, and hiding bodies meant that they stayed hidden. But the Trish of this lifetime believed in making nice with new neighbors for her husband's sake—for Darwin's sake.

She slid on some black, fluffy house shoes and let herself out onto the porch.

"It's okay, sweetie," the man coaxed, wrapping the woman's hand with a t-shirt he must've pulled from their luggage.

They walked to the minivan where he helped her inside.

She winced. "Ow. Ow. *Ow.*"

"Hey. I'm sorry to intrude, but I saw the whole thing. Here." Trish handed the cluster to the man, who gently placed it over the woman's hand. Blood soaked through the t-shirt and paper towels. Trish pressed her tongue against the roof of her mouth, and she bit the inside of her moistened cheek. The smell was reminiscent of the juices from amazingly well-seasoned smoked meat, but it was blood from what could've been a healthy middle-aged woman. Not too sweet. Not too salty, but just right.

Soon, she thought.

"Thank you so much," he said after buckling his wife in. "Uh, I'm Pete Morgan, and this is my wife—"

"Cecilia," his wife interrupted. "And I'm sorry, but we have to go." Her shoulders trembled, and she sucked air between her clasped teeth. She held her wrapped hand and rocked.

"Oh, okay. Well, I'm Patricia, and I'm always here to help."

Pete nodded and headed over to the driver's side.

Cecilia blew hard through bared teeth. "Oh God, hurry," she belted as they pulled out of the driveway.

Trish looked down at the puddle of blood on the sidewalk. It pooled into a chilling splotch. She wanted to get on all fours and lap it up like a dehydrated dog. But she didn't. Instead, she sighed and went back across the street. Back inside.

In the entryway, her heart leapt as Darwin's cries filled the house. She hustled over to the office. "Mommy's coming, bear," she announced.

"Momma," he called for her.

Her heart melted, and she rushed for the boy with open arms. She picked him up and shushed him while rocking him gently over her shoulder. He calmed down straightaway and wrapped his arms around her neck.

PART 4

Preparations

CHAPTER 11

Maggie

Trish watched Maggie climb out of her navy Prius, her dark hair freshly curled and ivory skin glowing in whatever foundation she was trying out. But as Maggie strode across the yard, Trish couldn't help but think, *Miller*. She shrunk, feeling a new pressure. With that, she moved from the curtains and headed for the door.

Darwin rode around in his walker, stomping about, breaking in his little legs. She smiled as he toddled by, cutting off her path. Then she frowned, wishing she could stay home and watch him, catch his next new stride in action. But she couldn't.

She had to go to Miller: the scene of something horrific that was still raw and open: an unsolved mystery for Miller, and an unhealed scab in Trish's short repertoire of loose ends.

Trish pulled the door open, her heart fluttering. She thought carefully about the night ahead. *How am I going to feed? Where can I look first? What's going on in Miller tonight anyway?*

Maggie clutched her phone in one hand and uneasily climbed up the steps, carefully looking down as if afraid she'd lose her footing. Or careful not to scuff her stark-white tennis shoes. The girl carried a mini leather backpack over her thin shoulder and wore holey jeans, exposing her knees and some of her thighs. Her short jacket hugged her slender waist.

Maggie was no different from most teenagers; she only cared about things that had no real value. She always showed up with

63

something new and trendy that she kept clean for a few months before placing it with something else.

"Hey, Mrs. Weston," Maggie said, a delightful smile crossing her face.

"Hi, Maggie. Thanks for coming over after such short notice," Trish started. "Randel had to—"

"It's totally fine. I really missed the little guy."

Do you miss Darwin? Or is it time for new clothes, makeup, weed or shoes?

Darwin fussed as she strolled inside. He walked over and reached toward her, beckoning Maggie to pick him up. She slid her phone in her back pocket, and pulled him out of his stroller, sitting him on her hip. "I—"

Darwin grabbed a handful of her thick, curly hair and shoved it into his mouth. She winced. "Ow!" she exclaimed, her dimpled cheeks fading into a frown.

Trish rushed over and gripped his small hands. "No, no, no," she said, unraveling Maggie's hair from around his short fingers.

"Ow! Gosh, Darwin." Maggie went red in the face. Then, after looking at Trish and maybe seeing the embarrassment or surprise that matched her own, she laughed. "Are you hungry?" she asked through a watered-down giggle.

"No," Trish said. "He shouldn't be. He just had a bottle, and I even put oats in it."

"Oh well, I'll be sure to feed him in an hour or so. Isn't that right?" Maggie asked him after he rested his gripping hand on her shoulder. He smiled.

He isn't the only one who's hungry, Trish thought, fighting to curb her own cravings. Her stomach growled in response.

Indiana would've been perfect. The last body she'd scouted out there had been found in a well and the death had been ruled as an accident. The man had simply been out drunk and fell on his neck. The heat from the authorities was nonexistent, and no one was looking for her...there.

She couldn't say that much about Miller. Victoria Scott had been reported missing. Not dead.

Darwin growled and yelled, frustrated with Maggie for cooing at him as she used her free hand to pick up his walker. Trish wondered what he was trying to say. She followed Maggie into the living room and watched her sit Darwin back inside it.

"I'll be back between eleven and midnight," Trish said.

Maggie headed for the kitchen.

"All right, that's fine," Maggie said, tussling with what sounded like a bag of Cheesy Puffs. She reappeared with Darwin's favorite snack.

"Call me if you need anything. I won't be too far away."

Please, don't call me, Trish thought, hating having suggested it in the first place. The last thing she needed was a distraction. She worried about Darwin, naturally, but there was no need for her paranoia to have her watch her phone for an anticipated emergency when there never was one. She could give Maggie that much. Darwin was never sick or hurt when left in her care. Just a little tired and over-sugared. Trish always smelled pop and candy on him.

Secretly coming to terms with the plan for the evening, Trish decided heading out sooner than later was ideal. "Well, I probably don't have to state the obvious, but Darwin's been ornery all day. Sorry if he decides to give you more of a hard time than normal." Trish picked up her keys, purse, and duffle bag from the couch.

"Oh, that's no problem, Mrs. Weston. Darwin's my little buddy. Yeah? You my little buddy?" Maggie poured the cheese puffs on his walker's table. She bent at the waist and brushed a knuckle over Darwin's plump cheek. "He's never a problem."

The boy giggled and blushed. Then he banged his small fists against the cheese puffs before shoving a handful in his small mouth.

The women laughed.

"If I feel like I won't be back by eleven, I'll call you. The girls from my class like to turn yoga into a full-fledged night out sometimes. And it's been a while, so…"

"I totally understand. And that's fine. I'm sure you could use a break. And like I said, Darwin has never been a problem. I love hanging out with this little guy." Maggie paused and then raised a finger. "Oh yeah, can you do me a favor? Can you let Mr. Weston know that

I got a good grade on that essay that he helped me with?" She smiled. "I texted him, but he never responded."

"Really? What'd you get?" Trish asked. Just a couple of weeks before, Randel had helped the girl with her essay, fearing she wasn't doing well at school. He had a weird care for her. Not in a perverted way, but in a leader-of-the-community way. He was concerned when their neighbor's yard overgrew, incidentally finding out that Mr. Pepper moved to Florida, leaving Mrs. Pepper to fend for herself. When Dr. Claud missed his daily jog for a week, Randel found out that he had a cardiac arrest, dying in the house across the street. He was an all around good guy, nothing like her.

"I got an eighty-two percent. Without his help, it would've been a zero, because honestly, I didn't plan on turning it in. I mean, who cares about the French Revolution? It was a long time ago." She tossed a cheese puff in her mouth. "But yeah, anyways, he taught me a lot, and I passed. I figured he should know." She chewed, crunching on *Darwin's* snack.

Trish chuckled. "What? You don't care about school? Isn't that the point of this gig? To help you pay for it?" Trish felt that she knew the answer. Maggie's parents, Mark and Bianca, paid for college. But Trish humored her anyway.

"Being stress-free is a happier way to be. Things have a way of working out for me, so I just leave it to the universe." Maggie turned to Darwin. "Right, little monster?"

Trish's heart dropped to her belly, and she stared hard at Maggie. Her carefree smile and laxed stance was bordering on irritating. But instead, she looked away. *She didn't mean anything by it. Relax,* she told herself. *The stupid girl doesn't know that the real monster is standing right here, ready to pounce. I mean, why even go out? Why not just…* Trish refocused her mind on an actual plan, one that made sense.

Miller University. She had to see what the campus was like that night. It had only been two months since she was there, and there was barely any time to plan. Regardless, she had to eat.

"Stay out as long as you want. My brother's in town, and it's *way* too loud at my house with him rehearsing for his shows and having all types of people come by. My parents even abandoned ship for the week. I'll be up all night watching *The Love Room*." Maggie's face lit up. "They just released the new season, and it's really long and I heard it was *so* good!"

Trish nodded and slid her coat on before heading for her son. Darwin met her with his big dark eyes and smiled. Then, he picked up a soggy chip and offered it to her.

CHAPTER 12

Southern Luna

As Trish drove into the dying afternoon, she entered the waking evening. As usual, her small village of Lakeshore was on par for a chilly, quiet suburban night. The houses, both tri-level style and traditional, belonged to retirees, single professionals, and full families who worked in the Lakeshore District, Industry Row, or downtown where they tended to the tourists who crowded the area every summer. The docks stayed active as businesses welcomed the fishers of Lake Michigan with their twenty-pound lake trout and king salmon. In the summers, the waters warmed in the blazing sun, beckoning the introverts from their winter cubbies and the extroverts to show off their newness after a long winter of bar hopping, meetings, and vacationing down south or on some elite island. Her town had some of the best beaches in the Midwest and was a haven for the biggest serial killer in human history; but the town rested easily.

Never eat where you sleep, she thought.

She watched private jets cut through the sky, landing at a private airport for the richest among the people. Ironic, because the smallest houses and the biggest families lived nearest the airport. Sometimes, it baffled her that people would put up with the noise from the airport that they could never afford to use. If their tight budgets allowed, they would pack their families into their van and make the forty-five-minute drive to the Grand Rapids airport instead. She sighed, wondering why she thought of those people at all. It was funny how some of the rich loners in town just knew they were better off than those people in the small houses by the airport, when in turn, if she was the monster she had been in the beginning, those rich loners would be on the top of her list of potential victims simply because of their seclusion.

Whenever she got the chance to think back, she did, and although she regretted it at times, it was a necessary exercise.

In the late 1890s, she was sure she would be caught. She was sure that some town in some mountainside or forest would spot her, know what she was, and kill her on the spot. But she had gotten lucky. She had something that others, if there were more like her, probably didn't have: the alchemist, the serum, and the will to continue. She silently thanked her ambition and then flushed at the thought of giving herself a literal pat on the back. If there were others like her, how were they surviving in this age? She was smart enough to go and learn how electronics worked and how they advanced. She knew most inventions and read patents like books. She even printed them out and read as she hunted. She knew about blood diseases and made a catalogue in her journal.

Trish frowned as the downtown brick luxury apartments turned into the main stretch. Flat grasslands flew by on either side and traffic became scarce. The four-lane road adopted a median, pulling the opposite direction of traffic farther away from her side of the road. Streetlights were reserved for the gas stations that showed up every five miles until they showed up every ten, and the only company on the road was in the form of roadkill.

Going back into Miller so soon after Victoria Scott had been proclaimed to be a missing person made Trish's palms moisten as she squeezed the steering wheel.

Instead of looking forward to her meal for the evening, she ruminated on a video that she'd watched earlier that day. Even though the local police were too busy to investigate what happened in Chad's dorm room that night, the YouTubers were not. In fact, Trish counted eleven different channels who had about two to three videos each on the matter.

The one that she listened to the most, *Southern Luna True Crime Podcast*, was more thorough and accurate in most of the details. Her southern drawl sounded a lot like Momma's, oddly offering a level of comfort to an otherwise dastardly event that could end life as Trish knew if she were to ever get caught.

"This is a strange one, ya'll, and I need to do more research. But I really wanted to get this video out because we need to find this girl. She could still be out there, and she could help the police find a killer. Victoria Scott, also known as Vicky, is known for being a loving daughter and sister and excelled at school. She was a courageous advocate and protested oil and gas companies and fought for civil rights for under-privileged groups. Now, y'all, this is all the police released about the night she was attacked, but I feel like there is more to the story. I'll keep lookin' into it, but this is all I can find right now. Vicky attended Miller University. In her sophomore year, she was at a fraternity party with a friend who told her to go inside and get something for her. When Vicky went inside, she saw a classmate being attacked by a woman with a knife, who then turned and attacked Vicky. The classmate, Chad Reid, was pronounced dead at the scene with multiple stab wounds to his chest."

Trish rolled her eyes. The police lied to the public on a regular basis. She would never stab anyone to death—what a mess that would be.

Southern Luna went on:

"A girl who had been on the phone in the next room heard a struggle take place in Chad's room and alerted the fraternity brothers who had been downstairs drinking and partying with many other students. This is probably why the assailant was able to get inside the house and kill Chad without anyone noticing. I don't know, let me know what y'all think in the comments."

True, Trish thought, but she didn't dare leave her thoughts in the comments section.

"By the time Chad's fraternity brothers broke in, the killer was gone, and Vicky was on the floor unconscious with a stab wound in her neck. That's also kinda strange because why didn't the killer stab her more than once? And did she walk in on the attack, or was she already in the room? Because the fraternity brothers said they had to break the door down. Anyway, Vicky was rushed to the hospital where she stayed for four days. Now, her family wasn't allowed to go in and see her, and the staff at the hospital told reporters that the federal government was lurking around, trying to ask Vicky questions, but I guess they never got a chance because she was in a coma the whole time. But one day, a nurse went to check on her, and she was gone."

Trish froze, having known that Victoria was missing, but *also* knowing that Miller should have been out of bounds for her night out. But she was desperate and convinced that Victoria had to have been dead by then.

"Her belongings were gone; her phone was gone...it was like she was never there. The police released a sketch of the killer..."

Ugh, Trish thought. She'd been listening to the video, but she picked up her phone to look at the screen. The sketch looked like a pale alien with large eyes and high cheek bones. The hair looked nice, thick, dark, and lush as it fell onto her shoulders. If they wanted to find whoever was in that picture, then they could go watch the *X-Files*. She shook her head. It looked like none of the idiots at the party had seen her at all. She chuckled as Southern Luna continued.

"And here is the latest picture of Vicky." Trish cocked her head but was not at all surprised that it was a dead ringer for the girl. Even light brown skin, average build, honey eyes, and long crinkly hair. Trish's heart loomed in her chest. That was Victoria Scott alright. She was wearing the same tank top and jean shorts she had worn that night. Trish imagined Victoria posed for that picture on that fateful day.

The day I thought I killed her.

"The police combed all of Miller, searched dorm rooms, cricks, Lake Michigan, Grand River, surrounding farmland, and the woods, and found nothing. Just like the attacker from that night, Vicky vanished. If you know anything about the attack that night, have a lead on the attacker, or have seen Vicky, please call this number."

The number that popped up was local, leading with a 616-area code.

"Or go over to the Facebook page and the website, FindVictoriaScott.com, that her family and friends put up. They are very active over there, and always willing to take tips around the clock."

The idea of Victoria's body never being found left Trish uneasy. She flushed, almost welcoming the euphoric sense of heat to wash her face, a sensation that only the ring allowed her to feel. But then she remembered what the reaction meant. She was nervous. Where was Victoria's body? Did she turn? Or did someone else do away with her?

When Trish left West Virginia, she staggered off into the woods and was never seen again either. Once she made it to New York, she took up a room in a boarding house with European immigrants. When they went to work in the factories, she went to the library, thanks to the ring. The library was the perfect place for her in the 1890s because it didn't smell too much like people. It smelled like withering paper and old trees. Black ink and dust. The smell was welcoming, taking Trish's mind off the smell of musk and sweat.

She spent her days pulling up newspaper articles from her small Appalachia village. They were easier to find than she thought; the librarian ordered them whenever Trish asked for them. The photos of the carnage in the chicken coop were on the first page of *Hopkins Daily*. There was blood everywhere. Chicken parts all over. There was blood where she had been bitten, but there was nobody. There were footprints that led outside and into the woods, but the dogs could not pick up a scent. There were so many holes and black boxes around the situation that they had no choice but to hope she'd turn up one day, dead or alive.

But there she was, one hundred and thirty-seven years later, heading east toward the scene of a crime, just to prepare to commit another.

CHAPTER 13

Storage

Trish pulled into the Stow-Away parking lot. Just fifteen miles south of her lakeside town, the storage facility was useful and immediate, always on the way but also very out of the way. It sat alone on Interstate 5 in the middle of the modest farm town of Frameton, with the nearest gas station being twelve miles north, just off the highway.

The short, two-story tower sat on the west side of the mini complex's parking lot, and a slew of outdoor storage containers extended next to the tower, against the north side. The man, Earl, was working in the front office. His head stayed still while his eyes focused on something in front of him. Trish was certain it was the television. She'd stored there for years, and if one thing didn't change, it was Earl's watching his shows.

Gray-haired, with tight eyes and a prominent frown, Earl couldn't care less about her, a predator who had lived out of one of his units over the last eight years. He'd never been a problem, and she was sure he never would be.

"Nah," Trish teased, convinced his presence was comforting. Earl was the only person she'd ever seen there, and she hoped it'd stay that way.

She backed her jeep into a well-lit parking spot around the back of the tower, a few spots away from the rear door. Then she climbed out, locked up, and headed toward the back entrance, inhaling frosty air. Her stomach squirmed and cried, begged and buckled.

After walking through the backdoor, she rushed up the steps, careful to listen but only hearing the buzzing light fixtures that offered nothing but dimness, which was fine with her: less for the cameras stationed on the ceilings near a corner of each floor to see. On the second floor, she approached storage container 204, then crouched and disabled the combination lock: 9-23-23. She gripped the bottom of the door and pulled it up, allowing herself inside.

Trish pulled the door down behind her and stepped into the darkness. She reached to the right, tapped the cold base of a lamp sitting on a file cabinet, and flushed the space with a hard yellow light, illuminating the steel walls.

The life she'd buried in the storage container waited for her return. Her plushy red rug sat in the middle of the concrete floor. Her body mirror leaned against the opposite wall, facing her. She turned her nose up a bit, looking herself over before fixating on the glinting ring. Obsessing over its very existence was maddening.

Literally.

Before she could dwell any longer, she got back on course, quick to cure oncoming procrastination and useless pondering.

Trish pulled the top drawer of the dresser open and looked inside. Her choices weren't vast, but there certainly were options. As always, there was a dress code, depending on the hunting ground. She saved denim for the truck stops, silk for the singles bars, and cotton dresses for college parties. The dresses outlined everything, even her perky nipples and slender waist.

Yes, she thought, eyeing the olive, long-sleeved cotton dress folded neatly next to a glass jar she called "the canine collection." The dress stopped mid-thigh, and it fit her silhouette like a glove. *Cherry red lipstick…and those knee-high boots over there.* She went for the shoes organized on the bottom of her clothing rack, next to the mirror. Trish decided on the black suede ones with the clunker heels. She'd also chosen to throw on a different winter coat, although it looked a lot like the one she'd been wearing: black with faux fur around the brim of the hood. The coat hung next to an array of purses. She moved her wallet from the yoga tote to a leather purse, which was already equipped with lipstick, eyeliner, concealer, foundation, and a hand-sized mirror.

Perfect, she thought. She laid her outfit across the oak dresser and stopped. Guilt clenched her gut. She should've been home with her son—the life she had made and vowed to protect.

That's not my reality, she told herself, fighting back tears and denouncing the thought. *How can I protect him if I don't—*

"No," she grunted. "This is just like any other night. Darwin is fine. Darwin will be fine. Dar—" She caught herself in the mirror and said sternly, "Darwin is all right." She raised a brow. "You're not doing anything wrong *or* different. You are surviving. He *needs* you to survive." Trish took in a deep breath.

Once upon a time, shame would've trumped her completely. She used to wish she had died during those gruesome touches of death. It stalked her once or twice, begging for her capture or persecution. Hanging or incineration.

Sometimes, she'd even *hoped* they'd catch and kill her. Murder the beast. Make the monster extinct. She wouldn't have to fight and hide, kill and sneak. It would simply be over, and it had always been so exhausting.

But that didn't matter, because no matter how she felt sometimes, she still went out, she still ate, and she still killed. She still hid bodies and staged crime scenes. She still did the things that became her daily life. She was still Trish and, in that moment, standing there in the storage container, she was alive and she was hungry.

Trish pulled off her boots and put them on the shoe rack. Then she took off her yoga pants and sweater and shoved them in her duffle bag, leaving herself to stand in the middle of the storage unit in her silk black bra, boy shorts, and white cotton socks.

She pulled the second drawer open and grabbed a cluster of rolled-up t-shirts. A red ruffled hairband held the bundle together. She placed the cluster of cloth between her teeth and bit down hard.

Her nostrils flared.

Okay. Okay, she thought faster. *Okay, okay, okay, okay! Go!*

After a few shaken breaths, she quickly pulled the ring from her finger and slammed it onto the dresser top. Immediately, she felt her own blood slowing and freezing, her muscles shivering. Trish clutched the end of the dresser top, bracing for an all-too-familiar pain. She strained and heaved, the cramps running up her limbs and folding her gut. Her breath burst from her nose, and saliva soaked the cloth lodged between her teeth. Her body clenched and threatened to collapse under her. Trish hollered in her throat and flattened her hands, allowing her fingers to lengthen. Her skin burned as it faded pale, and her scalp screamed as her hair darkened.

Finally, Trish buckled at the knees and fell, accompanied by a heavy thud.

The soft, plush rug pressed against her convulsing figure. She lay on her side, brought her knees to her belly, and then straightened them out, hoping to ween off the gut-wrenching pangs. After a few seconds, the pain seemed to simmer down, so she slowly rolled onto her back and peered at the ceiling through blurry vision. Tears flowed down the sides of her face.

And then everything darkened.

Blind, she let out a muffled guttural wail. Her canines fell loose from her dilating gums, making room for a much thicker, sharper alternative. She bit harder and tasted cotton threads as her fangs penetrated the cloth. So did a mouthful of blood.

Trish swallowed hard and inhaled sharply, feeling her fangs retract and extend, solidifying space.

Almost over, she thought. *Almost over. Almost—*

Her heart thumped against her chest, shaking her body. The pain settled to minor aches, and she opened her eyes. A red haze layered the furniture and walls. Then a euphoric calm rode down the length of her body, restoring strength in her bones and skin. Clearing her vision. Numbing the pain and making her feel…better.

Trish pressed her hands into the rug and pushed herself up on her feet. She pulled the shirt from her mouth, ignoring the blood for the moment. She'd deal with it when it was time to clean up at the end of the night, which she hoped wouldn't be too late. She placed her discarded teeth into the jar and jostled it—the jar had about eight canines inside.

Need to get rid of this too, she thought.

She replaced the jar and stretched high; her bones cracked in response. Youthful energy and strength penetrated her old body, making her feel nineteen again. Trish's vigor wanted her to sprint through the West Virginian wilderness, duck and dodge low-hanging branches, and jump over boulders. She probably would have as a girl, but the energy had a different use tonight.

As the pain diminished to nothing, Trish picked up the olive dress. She put it on and adjusted it around her thin thighs. Then she stepped inside each boot, using the dresser top to hold herself upright. She grabbed the leather purse and stopped to look her appearance over once more. Her dark eyes were the best at hiding her true intentions because they weren't hers.

Trish missed looking into her own emerald eyes, the ones she was born with. But that was something she could never have back.

None of it would come back, because that girl was long dead.

CHAPTER 14

Miller, MI

As Trish pulled out of the Stow-Away parking lot, she failed to silence her heart's yammering. Her gut begged her to turn back. Find a safer place to hunt. Forget about Miller. But she'd already removed the ring and could only progress forward.

Quick and easy, she told herself. After reading about the events on campus that weekend—Homecoming, to be exact. It'd be simple to blend—worth the risk.

But with every ounce of optimism came a pound of worry; Victoria Scott was still missing. The girl should've resurfaced by then, alive or dead. There were only so many places the girl could've gone, and she was in bad shape the last time Trish, or anyone, had seen her. So where was she?

Trish shook her head because it didn't matter. Whether the girl was still missing or not, Trish was on her way to Miller University—the site of the one who got away.

She quickly timed the trip in her head. *It's forty miles away, and going the speed limit, it'd take...*

But her mind veered as she headed up the road toward the highway. Trish had scoured the internet, looking for any evidence or any follow-up to what she'd learned from Southern Luna. Trish only filled in a few holes: Victoria Scott was valedictorian of Cass Tech High School out of Detroit, Michigan...the second of two children...grew up in a Baptist church...secretary of the National

Honor's Society…and at the time she went missing, Victoria had been organizing a protest. The girl was literally putting together an effort to bus students over to West Michigan, Lakeshore of all places, to protest an oil refinery. There were many calls for her safe return all over social media because Victoria was involved, and people were out looking for her.

So where was this gem of a student?

Trish pondered, wondering if they'd found the body and couldn't identify it due to the wild animals in the area.

Did they find anything at all?

No, not the body of the boy, Chad. He had been instantly found in his bed, having bled to death from the wrist. And with no trace of her fast-degrading venom in the blood that remained, suicide had to be the only conclusion. Southern Luna didn't know that, and neither did the public. Trish did. But Victoria had disappeared without a trace.

Had to have bled out, Trish decided, wanting to get focused. *Had to have fallen out somewhere, and it's only a matter of time before they find her.*

The very thought made her quaver. *Blood.* There was so much food, so much to drink that night. Chad's blood had been warm and filling, and Victoria's was sweet and felt plentiful.

Trish's cheeks tingled as she merged onto the highway. Her tongue moistened, and her stomach growled, turning aches that made her shift. She could almost taste the sweet savory blood coating her tongue and sliding down her throat, filling her empty belly.

She imagined it felt a lot like Randel had felt when he took his first sip of red wine alongside a filet mignon and shrimp risotto, his go-to recipes. Humans were unique like that, having appreciation for different things. All her husbands had a favorite *thing* that brought on an energy that was wholly unmanageable, whether it be sex, alcohol, food, or work. Randel's was food and sex. After he finished his favorite meal, he'd lay her down and lick her between the thighs. A lovely, wet bliss that made her dizzy with ecstasy.

But only momentarily.

Sex and steak didn't quench *her* thirst. What she needed was far better. It was even better than Momma's warm porridge: grainy and sweet. Trish's taste buds tingled the same way they had back then.

She imagined herself curling her tongue around the warm stream of red, her teeth draining the unnatural opening. If her teeth didn't tear through the barrier, she'd snap her prey's neck, leaving it so broken that the bone would pierce the skin, making a blood waterfall.

Her chest tightened, and she watched the overpass overhead. Everything was dead, with very little traffic coming and going. The highway couldn't be any longer. Thick clusters of trees rose high on either side of the straight road before breaking into flat farmland. Dusk settled in, painting the familiar country road dark. But once she entered Miller, traffic swallowed the road, welcoming it onto Miller University's campus.

The party appeared to be in full swing. But Trish wasn't interested in the party because there were too many young people who rarely ventured out alone. Moving in groups, wasted off their asses and high on pills or weed, they'd ignore her advances and try to get her to take them to the liquor store instead. Though her true form was that of a nineteen-year-old woman, her make-up and clothes made her come off as a solid twenty-three. The kids would go as far as inviting her to some house for an after party, where the music was too loud, and time seemed to stand still. They'd get drunker, and she'd get hungrier and crankier.

The older ones, however, were done with the bland campus parties. They hung out at the twenty-one-and-up bars. Most didn't live on campus, and rarely did they have roommates because apartments were ridiculously cheap in Miller. Anyone with a single job could afford a one-bedroom apartment and a car note. To display their accomplishments, they rushed to mention such things over drinks, which made them easy victims to pick out.

And she'd always find them, except for last time.

New tremors crept up her spine. She looked around at the excited faces, deciding Victoria had to be long gone. Trish took in a deep breath and kept with her plan. *You're here now*, she thought. *Stick with it. Get in and get out.*

She turned right into Young's Bar and Grill. The parking lot had a few cars, but the place was dead, to say the least. Trish parked in the corner, in the blind spot of the camera whirring left to right just by the front door. Mastering her crafts—the innocent ones and the demonic ones—was tiring. Who knew keeping up with human technology would be a hassle? It was as if they evolved at an accelerated rate, making her figure out how to evade their inventions over and over again.

Luckily, she evolved with them.

Trish backed into the spot and looked around. The light had missed her, leaving a deep shadow over her car, just as she preferred. It'd appear as if she was never there. She opened her purse and pulled out the cherry lipstick.

As she watched herself fix her lips in the sun visor mirror, she considered her face. Alter egos were supposed to be stronger, offering a looking glass into the wormhole of an alternate existence. Patricia with the ring was nothing like that. She was another schmuck who worked for a living, took care of others, and cooked meals that she barely ate. Only thing was, she never died.

A depressing existence these people have. Living to die.

But it wasn't as bad as her own, reliving again and again, watching the circle of life take place, generation after generation: from Albert to Jacob, from Johnny to Mel, from Victor to Randel. Then Darwin.

A ball formed at the base of her throat. Tears rushed forward, just to be kicked back. Shaking the thought, she tucked it back into the crevices of her mind along with many other things.

She stepped out of the jeep and strutted up to the bar with heels hitting the pavement and boots that came up to her knees.

CHAPTER 15

Young's Bar and Grill

The late fall wind wrapped Trish, wisping through her hair. She bet it was chilly enough to wear earmuffs or a neck scarf. But she wouldn't know; she'd only bothered wearing her coat for show. Her body adjusted to the weather. Over a century ago, her body reacted to the climate; severe colds during the winter gave way to mild heat strokes in the West Virginian sun.

Trish's stomach turned a little as nostalgia threatened her with guilt. *What if Momma was alive to see this?* she thought. *She'd probably tell me to go be with my kid.* If a bullet to the chest didn't take Trish out, as it almost had in the past, depression brought on by the girl she used to be surely would. But those useless thoughts, too, were pushed aside.

Strawberry-coated nicotine collided with her face as she drudged past a few guys with long beards who were huddling close and passing around one of those e-cigarette vape things. Their knit caps and sport coats failed to protect them from the fall breezes. They all shivered or put their hands in their pockets, patiently awaiting their turn to pull on the sweet vapor. Even with the vapor suffocating the space, Trish caught a hint of burning wood, roasted meat, and cigar smoke. *They've been out for a while,* she thought, imagining them all sitting around a dinner table at some high-end restaurant. One of them stared hard and nodded at her. She smiled and pulled the door open, letting herself inside.

A typical dive bar, the sweet smell of spilled whiskey and standing dish water stuffed her nose. Trish swaggered past the cluster of wood furnishings and pulled out a stool that looked a lot like the chairs congesting the center of the small establishment—bruised and stained with age. Many a drunk had plopped down at that bar before she graced it. She looked around and was instantly pleased. In the far corner, closest to the door and near the tinted window, were a few young guys who sat with eyes plastered to their bright phone screens. One chuckled and showed the guy next to him what he'd been watching. They both laughed.

Tacky Christmas lights hung from the ceiling, nearly blocking the view of the top shelf—the only shelf stocked with liquor. The other shelves were packed with red plastic cups and small bags of potato chips with a handmade sign next to them stating: *$2.00.*

Trish smirked. Even if she were interested in eating potatoes drenched in oil, she wouldn't pay two bucks for them. She unzipped her coat but opted to leave it on as she slid onto the hard wooden barstool.

A middle-aged man with a face etched with age and disappointment trudged to the bar. He nodded and passed by Trish to get to the farthest end, and she nodded back. His scent was enough to send her on a sugar high. Hundreds of grams of sweetness pumped from his heart and mixed in with his blood. It reminded her of burning cotton candy. Diabetes blood was syrupy and thick, loaded with sugar. It was enough to make her teeth ache once.

The guys at the table perked up when the cluster of hipsters came through the door. Like long-lost friends, they passed hugs and excited jabber.

Trish searched their faces. They were young, but not too young. Some of them might have been fresh out of college. With them all standing so close together and several yards away from the bar, it was impossible to pick up their smells. Still, they were all fine candidates for the perfect meal. One of them was wide enough to fill her for the month. Maybe even two.

"Hey, Benny!" The bartender, maybe in her early twenties, approached the middle-aged gentleman with sugary blood. She was petite with dark silky hair and skin that reminded Trish of the wheat fields through the Great Plains. The woman could have been a descendant of the ancient pharaohs—according to modern renditions anyway.

"Hey, Sam," Benny replied.

Sam turned and yanked a pop refrigerator open. She pulled a navy-blue bottle from the top shelf on the far left and spun around. "How was the doctor? That was today, right?" The door shut with a soft thud.

"Yeah." Benny let out a heavy sigh. "He said my blood sugar is out of control and that I need to stop drinking."

Surprise, surprise, Trish thought.

Sam's face crumbled as she popped the lid off his beer. *Tsk.* "*What?* No." She placed a napkin in front of him and set the beer on it.

"That's what *I* said." He brought the beer up to his thin lips and sipped. "You wanna know what else I told him?"

Sam tilted her head up, humoring the man. "What'd you tell 'em?"

"I told him that if drinking is the death of me, that's fine. At least I'll die doing what I love. Just like he likes to suck money from my pockets just to sit there and tell me—a grown-ass, working man—what to do."

"Oh, Benny," Sam said, and they laughed. "How are your kids taking the news?"

Another bluster of laugher dragged Trish's eyes back to the table of guys. They cackled and chatted like they hadn't seen each other in ages. Words like "finals," "major changer," "MCAT," "oaths," and "after party" floated across the room.

Reassured, she knew where to go if the bar didn't pan out, because the night definitely wasn't ending with Benny, the man with candied syrup coursing through his veins.

One of the men rose from the table and made his way by her. His green eyes moved frantically, trying hard to avoid hers. She winked at him when he finally looked up. His pasty cheeks blushed, but he smiled back and tucked his hands in the fronts of his jean pockets.

Bashful looked cute on him.

Trish's eyes went soft, studying him, from his short dark hair to his taut arms, down to his tennis shoes. But it wasn't his boyish face or sheepish smile that set her heart racing. It was his rare, clean, mouthwatering scent.

CHAPTER 16

Locals

His musk was as sweet as a cherry blossom coated in honey. Trish's fangs leaked; the warm venom, flavorless on her tongue, drenched her mouth. She swallowed it, pretending *his* sweet life nectar had been mixed in. She'd fill up on him slowly just to savor his beautiful blood.

There was no way someone could be as pure…as clean…and young? Baffled, she smiled, trying to read him. Trying to *know*.

Could his blood really be that…divine?

He was new and as refreshing and pure as the sweet corn she and Momma would trade eggs for in the town square. Longing pulled her into another time. The spring air encompassing Skinner's Gap caressed her plump cheeks, and she took in the breeze passing through beds of mountainside blue and yellow quaker-ladies.

His pungent scent lingered around his aura, making her belly grumble. He brushed past, and she watched him. A faint smile hung on his face.

Trish searched his short frame—about five foot seven—and admired his husky build. He probably spent time at the gym. A gold rosary hung around his neck—he was a prayer. A hoper.

God can't save you tonight, Trish thought, imagining herself draining him and leaving him to be found by a friend.

"What can I get ya?" Sam asked. She rolled up her sleeves and rose an eyebrow. Her eyeliner made her hazel eyes look like a curious cat.

"Water for now," Trish said, trying to hide her frustration. She hated interruptions. They prolonged her very necessary process: scoping. And she'd found the one.

"Comin' right up." Sam turned her back to face the shelves. "Any—"

"As a matter of fact, I'll take a Cosmo," Trish said, hoping to keep the girl busy long enough not to continue the conversation.

"Coming right up. Any preference in vod—"

"The most expensive you have."

Sam reached high and grabbed a skull-shaped glass bottle from the shelf. It wasn't the best brand Trish ever pretended to drink, but it was close enough. Miller was a college town, after all. The liquor at the bars was subpar, since most students lived on tight budgets. Trish was sure the bartender was surprised she didn't have to pour off another shot of what smelled like pure ethanol.

Sam turned back and set the bottle on the bar. Then she headed to another refrigerator, this one with a *Balls Energy Drink* sticker plastered across the top in blue and yellow letters. She pulled out an off-brand cranberry juice, along with an orange bottle of triple sec from beneath the counter. "You in town for homecoming?"

"I'm sorry?" Trish searched for the face of the refreshing, pleasantly sweet man—nothing like Benny, who smelled like burned marshmallows. She could still smell the man, but she couldn't see him. Maybe he'd gone to the bathroom.

She turned to the bartender, or Sam, who looked at Trish with glassy eyes.

"Well, I've never seen you around here before. Not even on campus. I was wondering if you were here for homecoming. Most people are. And it's a big game tonight too. We're playing Michigan, and last I heard, we were down by fourteen points. I haven't seen this many alumni since we went toe-to-toe with Indiana two years ago."

"Oh, yes. I graduated from here a long time ago," Trish replied. *Damn you for all the stupid questions*, she thought. But she carried on with the conversation. *No need for her suspicions.*

Sam poured the mixture into a chalice with ice chunks and shook it. "Oh no, you don't look a day over thirty. Couldn't have been *that* long ago."

"Thank you. People always tell me I look young for my age." *Because I do look young for my age.*

"You *do*." Sam smiled and poured the drink through a stainless-steel filter and into a plastic cup. "Sorry, we don't have martini glasses. Most of our customers are too young to know what a martini is, or simply don't have the balls to hold it down."

"That's okay, sweetheart." Deep down, she was grateful. Pretending to drink from a plastic cup was much easier to hide than with a glass.

"Eight dollars," the bartender said.

Trish dug into her purse and placed a ten-dollar bill on the bar top. "Keep the change." It was the only cash she had on her that night, and she didn't plan on carrying anymore.

"Thanks."

"Busy night?" Trish asked.

"Not really. No one other than the Betas. But they always come here."

Trish smirked. "Well, I guess I'm infiltrating." She put her Cosmo to her lips, making sure not to take any into her mouth, then swallowed air.

"Nah. Those guys couldn't care less about that. Give them a couple more rounds and they'll be trying to get up your dress soon enough."

"You know them all?"

"Yeah, well. Everyone but him." Sam peered toward the men's room.

The man with the beautiful musk came back by the bar, taking a different route between the empty tables toward the cluster of men.

"Well, I'd say he's the most adorable of the bunch," Trish said.

"Yeah? What makes you say that?"

"Well, he looks like the most mature one of the group."

"Hm, I guess. But he's a bit short for my taste and…" She gazed down as if picking her next words carefully. Then she shook her head. "Nah, he's definitely not my type." Sam leaned in, and Trish held a gag in her throat. The bartender's blood was diluted with nicotine and cocaine judging by the vinegary smell wafting from her pores. *No wonder she's so thin,* Trish thought.

"But that guy he's talking to should be the one you go after. His dick is as long and thick as a container of tennis balls."

Trish narrowed her eyes. "How do you know?" She took a fake sip from her cup.

"Let's just say he never goes home alone. And when there is no one here to take, he goes after me." Sam winked.

"That's fair." Trish believed as much, even though that guy looked sweaty and thick. Sam was petite and could get anyone, especially him.

Sam looked over Trish's shoulder. "Looks like you got their attention."

Trish snuck a peek. The man's friend pointed a meaty finger at her, and they spoke underneath the excited group's banter. Both men had their eyes trained on her.

The man with the beautiful smell smirked, then swaggered over.

CHAPTER 17

Toby

"Is anyone sitting here?" he asked. His boyish face brightened with his radiant smile.

"You." Trish smiled.

He slid onto the barstool. "I'm Toby, and you are?"

"Trish," she said softly, drowning in his aura.

He put out a hand and shook hers. "Nice to meet you, Trish."

His skin felt warm, and his aroma could've dragged her into a wet red room for two. They'd hide from the world until he was no more and she was full. But she held it together, needing to know more before feasting.

Toby smiled back, then turned to Sam, who'd been emptying a bag of ice into the sink behind the bar. "An ice water please," he said. "And a—" He looked to Trish.

"Another Cosmo."

"Coming up," Sam said, before turning to fill the order.

"So, no drink?" Trish asked, knowing the answer. Toby's blood was as pure as a child's. No way had he been drinking alcohol, smoking weed, or doing any drugs, for that matter. He was all clean.

"No. I have a *natural high,* as the guys like to call it."

"Mm...I've never heard of that. A natural high?"

"Yeah. It's a blessing, really. No need for drinks or cigarettes or drugs. I get high on air, I guess. I've seen alcohol and narcotics destroy too many lives." He lifted a hand to Trish. "No offense."

"I'm not the one who's offended." She pointed at Benny, who had been scowling at the back of Toby's head for a few seconds now.

Toby turned to face the older man.

"You shouldn't go around judging people," Benny snapped.

"Oh, no, uh, Benny, I didn't see you there. I'm—"

"No! You shouldn't go around dogging people, just like everyone else in this fucking town," Benny snarled.

"Mr. Yellen, please. I didn't mean to—"

"I deal with enough of that shit from my kids. I don't need it from a self-righteous pastor! You hear me?" Benny stood and snatched his coat from the back of his stool. "I'm not *apologizing* for drinking. Whether I'm sick or not, you don't have the right to pass judgement on *anyone!*" He slammed a few dollars on the counter. "I'm not standing for it, Toby!" He stomped off, allowing the door to slowly close behind him.

The rest of the bar seemed to ignore the show or refused to stop their conversations to see what was going on. *Small towns,* Trish reminded herself. *Everyone knows what to expect from everyone. Strike one for the pastor.* She stopped herself from rolling her eyes, more disappointed than worried.

Sam sighed and shook her head, setting the drinks on the countertop. She put her hand on her hip. "You're not going to scare everyone off, are you?"

Toby raised his hands and sighed. "No. No. I'm here with my frat brothers. And I wasn't judging him. I'd never offend anyone in any way…intentionally."

Sam raised a brow. "All right then." She passed the bar and went for the table full of guys who hooted and hollered. Some of them even yelled her name.

"Anyway. I didn't offend you, did I?" Concern crossed Toby's face.

If Trish were a natural woman, she would've thanked him for the drink and kept looking for the next guy to buy round number three. Church men were overbearing with their beliefs and expectations. Yet she was everything but normal, and she was famished.

"It'll take more than that to offend me," she said.

"Well, that's good to know." He lifted his drink to her. Their cups met.

"You're a preacher at his church?" she asked, wanting to offer some sort of comfort. A rattled prospect would only make a messy feast.

"Yeah—over at Hope United. Well, I haven't seen Benny in a while, but his family is heavily involved in the church."

"So, you're a celebrity around here?" She felt her heart tumble down to her gut. "That's exciting." *People would look for him sooner than later...*

Toby smiled. "Well, I'm not the main pastor. I'm more of a junior preacher."

"That's why you don't drink... What brings you out here tonight?" *A preacher and a monster meet at a bar...*

"Ah, well, my fraternity brothers pulled me from my house. It's been years since I spent time with them, and even longer since I stepped foot inside a bar."

"Years?"

"Well, yes. Since right before graduation." Toby chuckled and shook his head. "It's been ten years. Where does the time go?"

"Oh really? Are you not a student?" Shocked, she studied him again, noting the youthfulness in his chiseled jaw line, dreamy eyes, and strong healthy blood.

"No. I finished my PhD a few years back, and now, I teach English lit and philosophy courses over at the college. I'm working on bringing the School of Theology over as well. You wouldn't believe how busy work keeps me."

"A bit young to be a professor and a preacher, aren't you?" *At least the youngest I've ever seen.*

He scrunched his face. "Well, I'd like to believe that I'm doing well to be thirty-three."

Trish nodded as her plan withered. She wasn't prepared to associate with a man of his caliber. These kinds of guys were independent and smart. Clean and well-rounded. And typically, she'd steer clear of the religious types because they always wanted her burned or decapitated…or stabbed in the chest. Unwanted memories threatened to surface, and she cringed.

"That's really good for you. Seriously. I know your family must be proud," she said.

He frowned. "Yeah, well, at least they *pretend* to be."

"That's all that matters, right?" She smiled frankly.

"Amen to that."

They clacked plastic cups.

"Do you live close to campus, Professor?"

Toby blushed. "Oh, don't call me that. I'm not at work or at the church. I'm out chatting with a beautiful woman."

"Oh, I'm sorry. *Toby*," she teased.

"And of course. It's easy to get there on my bike or just by walking. But tonight, since it's a little cold and the guys are drinking, I decided to drive. I mean, for all I know, the guys might drag me over to the city like in the good ol' days."

"Hm." Feeling the conversation going nowhere, Trish changed the subject. "Is there a lucky lady in your life?"

"There was one. But not anymore." Shame covered his face. She wasn't sure if it was because she bothered to ask about another woman, or if he'd done something wrong that caused his relationship to be *not anymore*. "That's another reason why the guys dragged me out. Aside from it being homecoming and all, they wanted proof that I wasn't cooped up in the house, reading the Bible or anything like that."

"I'm not at all surprised by that."

"Which part?"

"That reading the Bible isn't just work, it's also a hobby."

"Sure is."

"Interesting," Trish lied.

Toby smiled. "Many people don't think that."

"Well, I do. I also think that you're the most interesting person I've run across in a long time." It was true in a way that he could never imagine. She grinned.

He raised a brow. "Is that true?"

Trish nodded.

As much as she loved the idea of taking him, Trish realized and accepted the truth: Toby was a bust. A guy like this was rare but came as a bundled deal she couldn't afford. Besides, there was no way he would take a strange woman home after first meeting her. She pulled her phone out of her purse and checked the time: *8:06 p.m.* It was getting late, and she needed to find someone else, fast.

Trish decided to let him down easily. "How about we exchange numbers and—"

"Would you like to come over?"

Her tongue froze in place. *Well, that was easy.* Her mouth watered and she clicked her tongue. "Are you sure? What about your friends?"

"They'll be fine. I can meet up with them later on. I'll drive us and then bring you back here."

Does he think I'm a prostitute? She quickly decided that it didn't matter if he did because the blood in his veins sang to her. Coaxed her to fall into its flow. And there was no time to waste. "Sure, uh, let me go to the restroom, and I'll meet you here?"

"I'll be waiting," he assured her.

Trish put her purse over her shoulder after rising from her seat. Then she slid her hands down her sides, adjusting her dress. She could feel his eyes on her as she headed to the bathroom, watching her figure, dreaming of her naked body. He wanted to feel and taste her on his tongue.

She smirked. No matter how God-fearing, every mortal man had a weakness. And she'd found Toby's. It wasn't beer or wine, cigarettes or weed, cocaine or heroin. Power or control.

It was *women.* How a thirty-something teaching preacher could be single was no longer a mystery. Toby was noncommittal because marriage could be dull for some people. Besides, why would he commit to anyone with so many young women around? Why should he want to go on and get married at all?

Perhaps his girlfriend left him for a good reason, she thought.

CHAPTER 18

Doubt

Trish headed inside a stall and locked it behind her. She opened her purse and refreshed her lips, adding another layer of cherry red lipstick using a personal mirror. She breathed in deep and stared at the back of the door, which was covered in makeup graffiti made of people's names, who had been there, and who was going to be with whomever else *4 life*.

Toby had probably fucked a student or two...or even banged a few women in the congregation. And he couldn't blame it on inebriation. It was *all* him.

Trish felt her nerves go unsteady as giddiness made her perk up. She wasn't prepared for the best meal she'd had in a long time: the blood of a preacher, the liquid of an established professor. She was set to gorge on a big member of the community.

What am I doing? She frowned, extinguishing her short burst of excitement. Typically, she'd run the other way. Peeple would look for him. He was out with people that he had known for years inside that very bar. Was it really worth the risk of getting caught? *Yes*, she thought, because she wouldn't get caught. She'd be long gone before anyone noticed. She wanted him and would have him.

He'd be delicious. The community would lose him, but they wouldn't know how, which was enough for her.

She felt herself getting excited again as her empty belly made the decision for her.

But they saw you together here, she bickered to herself.

So? That doesn't mean anything. They'd have to find him and my DNA, which…

The bathroom door opened, smacking the wall behind it. What sounded like a few girls barged in, giggling and drunk.

Foot traffic must be picking up.

"Oh my God," one girl said. "I can't believe she's doing it."

"I know. She's such a slut," another replied.

"I mean, he *is* cute though. And what are the odds that he'd be here?"

"I know, right? A professor? At Young's?"

"I mean, it makes sense. It's not like he's ancient, like Professor Houghton—"

"God's cousin."

"Or Dr. Monroe—"

"An actual fucking mummy."

They giggled.

"Right! Professor Webb isn't that much older than us."

"Oh, call me *Toby*," the girl deepened her voice, poorly imitating him.

"Or *whatever* the fuck… He's adorable, 'specially when he's up there at church! *Ugh*. I ignore Pastor Bennet and just stare at Toby, wanting to take him into the confession booth!"

"That'll be three Hail Mary's…"

"I'm just saying, if Gabby doesn't leave here with him, I will."

"Oh, bitch, please. You'd leave here with a used mop."

"Shut up!" a gleeful cry.

The girls laughed again.

Trish glowered. Not only were they stepping in her way, or trying to, she fought the urge to open the door to see their faces because they reminded Trish of herself and Mel. *A lot* of modern-day women sounded like Mel and Trish. They'd run into restrooms just to gossip about some guy they met at a music festival or truck stop. They'd make fun of men who got them high on acid—Mel actually took the stuff and Trish pretended—paid for their food, and then stormed off into the night when Mel and Trish flaked out on their end of a deal which was usually a threesome. Trish and her best friend had teamed up to charm strangers just to bask in their dismay over and over for years.

Melody.

Trish furrowed her brow, hating the sound of the long-dead woman's name in her memory. Mel's glossy orange hair and wide gap tooth smile hid the lies and betrayal that lived in her depraved mind.

Melody.

Focus, Trish shouted to herself, not sure why she thought of Mel more than normal lately.

Let's get going, she hyped herself up. She'd be damned if she had survived such a boring conversation with Toby for no reason. He was leaving with her, and he was going to die from her hunger.

Trish was sure of that.

***

On her way back to the bar, Trish spotted Toby. A young woman had her round face awfully close to his ear. Her long dark hair looked as if she'd washed it with glitter; the silver specks glistened in the dim bar which had filled up with patrons wearing any mixture of silver and blue. The game must have been over. Toby smiled and pulled away from her whispers. Then he looked at the bathroom to see Trish returning.

Don't flake on me now, bastard.

She relaxed when he rose from the stool and walked toward her, leaving the girl with a look of drunken confusion on her face.

"Ready?" Toby asked, hooking his arm out, welcoming her to latch on.

Trish wrapped her arm around his. He clenched his forearm and pulled her close.

CHAPTER 19

Ride

Trish exhaled the chilly air and watched the frosty cloud fade into the frigid night. Excited banter echoed along the streets. Students cheered, pouring off campus and onto Young's property.

Traffic had let up on the narrow road that Trish used to drive into town. Cars were going at a steady pace, with traffic both turning onto campus and driving past it. The parking lot started to fill in, with cars coming in to park, filling up the first several rows. A group of shirtless guys staggered across the parking lot, hooting and hollering, chanting and disrupting traffic. One car slammed on the brakes to let the group pass, sure to lean on the horn. But the men continued forward, never acknowledging the stopped cars who waited to park.

"I live pretty close, just on the other side of campus," Toby said. He pulled his jacket collar up, covering his ear lobes. "It's gotten *busy*. Hopefully, by the time I bring you back, there are less students out and about."

She snorted. "You mean when the bar closes?"

They laughed.

As the loud group approached them, one guy darted around the group and cut through the parking lot at top speed. He threw up his pale middle fingers and yelled, "Woooo! We are the fucking Warriors, bitches!"

The men from the group he left behind shouted in agreement. Once he reached the door, he carried his shouting inside of Young's.

Toby shrugged. "I guess that means we won the big game?"

"Maybe." She peered at her car across the parking lot. No way the camera could catch the license plate issued to Patricia Weston.

Humans and their technology. Almost every invention the mortals developed made her life, or lack thereof, more difficult. On top of the tiresome patent research, enduring debates, proposals, and reports, she'd spent almost a million dollars over the last century learning to disassemble and reassemble modern technology to find the work around. What she learned, mostly from common sense and experience, was that cameras aren't one hundred percent reliable; a lot of times, they didn't get a three-sixty view of the room or establishment they were tasked with securing. Also, a security system wasn't cheap. Since Young's didn't carry top-shelf vodka, Trish assumed the camera over the door was out of service too.

Toby wrestled with his keys, and the headlights of his dark Mustang lit up—also out of the camera's view. His car was parked three spaces away from hers.

He walked to the passenger side and opened the door for her.

"Thanks," she said, a little amused at the dated gesture. Men hadn't done that since…*the early nineties?* She sat inside.

"You're welcome. *Chivalry* isn't dead…yet." He winked before closing her door.

Trish watched him round the back of the car, heading for the driver's seat. Once inside, he started the engine and cranked the heat up. He rubbed his hands together and blew into his palms.

"Woo. It's a little bitter out. Is it too cold for you? You want me to turn up the heat more?"

Trish smiled. The cold felt like nothing on her skin. But to avoid questions about her odd body temperature, she'd worn an insulated jacket that kept her near ninety-six degrees—or at least the personal trials she'd run at the turn of the season, with a thermometer shoved between her cheeks, had assured her. Though with the chilly winds outside, she wasn't sure if she'd still feel cold to the touch tonight.

"Yeah. But I'm always cold. It's normal," she said, just in case. Trish zipped her jacket up more, bringing the collar over her chin.

"All right." Toby turned the knob, and heat blasted from the vents. She felt herself warm and then she felt nothing again. Toby shifted the car into reverse before pulling out to a red light. They watched students yell and scream joyously, filling the apartment parking lots lining the narrow street on either side. Some had glow sticks and plastic red cups, blue and/or gray wigs and football jerseys. Some didn't have shirts on at all, even in the dead of the cold evening. It was like watching a public rave.

All the potential witnesses made Trish shrink. Conflicted, she sighed to herself. Miller's condensed population was heavily preoccupied, which was a good *and* bad thing. Good because they were too busy celebrating in the streets to notice Toby, a dear *preacher* in town, was riding around with a dangerous stranger. Bad because Trish might not get back to her car undetected.

All the risks associated with the catch piled up, but hunger kicked her in the gut, making her midsection ache. Trish had to eat, or Lakeshore would have a ravenous beast on the loose. That wouldn't be good for anyone, especially Randel, Darwin, Pita, Trish's neighbors…

"Is this normal?" Trish asked.

"What?" He made a left onto a narrow street. A concrete sign arched over it, reading: *Miller University.*

"The students acting like this…?"

"No. We rarely win anything this big, and a win against Michigan is celebration-worthy. Trust me, they'll simmer down in a week. Midterms are coming up."

Spindly cypress trees embellished the curbs along both sides of the street, and cars lined up, bumper to bumper, hoping to exit campus in the opposite direction. All were stalled by a blue bus with the words *Grand Rapids* scrolling across the neon destination sign. People beat on their horns and hung out windows and sunroofs, yelling at ladies dressed in pumps and cocktail dresses who were slowly boarding the bus.

The emptying campus was bright, with yellow lights hanging from tall poles wrapped in silver garland. A brick clock tower stood tall at the end of the road. Behind it was a contemporary brick building that looked like a crooked stack of boxes. It reminded Trish of the block towers that Darwin would build before stomping them flat, just to turn around and build them again.

Trish and Toby followed the road as it curved left toward a host of brick apartments, where students threw tissue rolls onto parked cars. Toby stomped on his brakes when a thin, naked boy ran into the road. Several girls stood on the curb nearby, laughing at the boy's hairy bulge, which hung out for the wind to kiss and the world to see. He stuck his tongue out and put devil horns on his head with his index fingers and thumbs.

"Moron," Toby mumbled, blowing the horn.

The boy scampered off to chase the group of girls.

"Geez, I guess security got the night off," Toby complained. "That's a good way to get tossed in jail, bud."

Trish snickered. "Aren't you going to call the police?"

"What? Nah. They're just kids having fun. He'd just better hope he doesn't run into a cop, because the Miller Police...*sheesh*. They don't shy away from making an example, that's for sure."

What a pushover, she thought. *No doubt some of his students will miss him taking their side.*

"Anyway, I used to live there." He pointed to the side of the street closest to Trish. The building was like any other college dormitory. It was well kept, with trees and picnic tables out front and a lobby made of glass.

She raised a brow and smiled, elated at a new revelation. "Nice," Trish said, not regarding the apartment, but the massive construction site behind it. No one would find his body... "What's going on back there?"

"Ah. Yes. The university is expanding, as always. Remember when I told you about the School of Theology?"

"Mm hmm."

"Well, the new School of Education and Philosophy will feature the program. It'll be back there, along with a new student center and another admin building."

Toby turned left onto another narrow road, passing by a glass building standing high. The silver outline of the windowpane glinted in campus streetlights. The sign out front read: *Hugh Undergraduate Library*. Trish briefly watched a couple of students who sat alone against the windows on the first and third floor, their heads bowed, maybe reading or studying.

The winding street wrapped around the library and ended at a stoplight. They faced a thick wall of trees and an adjacent street, everywhere dark around them. The campus streetlights only lined their side of the road, barely illuminating the other side.

"Almost there," Toby said.

Good, she thought, cataloging her way back to her car. It was getting complicated.

PART 5

Blood Lust

CHAPTER 20

The Preacher's House

They pulled into a two-car driveway and stopped short of the garage door. The attached sky-blue Colonial sat on a stony foundation that seemed bright in the infinite blackness of Toby's street. Surrounded by foliage and slightly desolate, the nearest neighbor appeared to be about 1000 feet away. Toby's neighborhood maintained much of its forest, and his front yard lay hidden beneath the thick shadows of the tall trees.

"Home sweet home," Toby said, turning the car off.

Trish found herself impressed. He had a really nice house with lots of land on either side—much too big for one person, but big enough for no one to hear him scream should there be time for one to slip past his lips.

"You live here alone?" she asked as he let her out of the car.

Toby led the way up the walkway to the porch. A motion sensor light kicked on, outing the deepness of the crimson front door. The yellow light scattered and danced on the frosty glass window which took up the space above the silver doorknob. Below the doorknob was a keypad.

"Uh, yeah. I mean, aside from my cousin who stops by every now and again." He approached the keypad, sure to stand in front of it, obstructing her view. It beeped, allowing them inside.

Fortified, she thought. *Great. The killer was allowed inside.* Trish imagined the reporters and police repeating that very fact. There was no way she was leaving his body behind. Toby was leaving with her.

He flipped a light switch next to the door and lit up the living room.

"Have a seat or look around," Toby said. "You can put your coat on the couch."

An L-shaped leather couch sat up against the far wall, with two matching chairs across from it. They were situated evenly and neatly around an oak coffee table. Trish placed her jacket and purse on the couch, and Toby switched on the flat-screen TV mounted over the stony fireplace. He had enough sitting room to accommodate an entire family, so why didn't he have one of his own?

To be sure, or to learn about Toby—just as she had for all her food—Trish surveyed the photos on the fireplace, lined up neatly on either side of the TV. There had to have been about twenty of them up there.

"You like those photos?" he asked, opening the closet next to the front door. "My family and I do lots of things together."

Trish smiled and nodded as she looked at the pictures, trying to guess the year they were captured. Family, maybe three generations of them, posed for proms, weddings, funerals, and reunions. There were birthdays, holidays, and beach days. And as Trish became more acquainted with the space, she found photos on the walls and the coffee table too. She imagined the event when Toby was a mere child wearing a cloak with a white and gold hood. In another photo, young Toby huddled with several men. They looked like a team getting ready to shout, "Ready and break," before dispersing from a huddle.

"You're adorable," she said.

"Thanks. Now, come on. Let me show you around."

Trish walked across the living room. Her thick heels planted deep into the soft rug with each slow, steady step. Her eyes widened with amusement at the pearly grand piano sitting in the corner near the dark sliding door. A deep love for a long-lost hobby arose, and she approached the instrument.

She brushed her fingers against the keys. The ivory's light trill sent a chill up her back. No matter the decade or the generation, the piano's mellow voice remained unchanged. After leaving her first husband, Albert, Trish had spent time alone. During that time, she immersed herself in the classics, enjoying Jelly Roll Morton and Aaron Copland before learning to play herself. Music made it all right to be alone. She'd also been dubbed the Loner Killer who ripped and ran through the Northeast and Mid-Atlantic area. The name was much deserved, having killed many people; she clocked the body count at eighty-four. Of those eighty-four bodies, the police had only found ten and identified four. But it was so long ago that conjuring up the long-lost memories from the years 1924 to 1945 meant she needed to sit at a piano again. And even though she loved the piano, the things that she'd done during those times were too dis-turbing to want to remember. She had to clean out the back seat of her Rolls-Royce Ghost—Joyce is what she named it— every day and she refused to get rid of it; it was one of her only memories of Albert.

Oh well, she thought.

Feeling Toby's lusting eyes, she turned to him and asked, "You play?" "No. It was my dad's." He headed for the kitchen, which was across from the piano in the open floor plan. Cabinets lined the walls, and a granite island sat in the center. It reminded her of her kitchen.

Such a cliché modern design.

"I'm sorry, *was* your dad's?" she asked. *One less person searching for your body.*

"Yeah. He's no longer with us."

"Oh, I'm so sorry to hear that." Trish frowned.

"No, it's okay. He lives on through us: the church, the family, me. He's in God's arms now. Although he is in a much better place, I tell him every morning that he's truly missed."

"That's comforting," she said, eyeing the small silver crucifix on the wall behind the piano.

"Would you like some wine?" he asked.

Trish cocked her head. "I thought you didn't drink?" She hated when her meals lied to her.

"I don't, but that doesn't mean I don't have wine for my guests."

Right. Guests. Trish knew every man had a weakness, no matter how holy he claimed to be. Who knew how many women had been there before her? But that was furthest from her worries. Time drew closer to midnight, and according to the digital clock on the TV, it was 9:07 p.m. Impatience and hunger nagged at her gut. It was time to eat.

Not yet.

"Sure. Red, please." Swirling it around in her cheeks didn't taste so good, but it was fun to pretend she filled her cup with the blood of her unsuspecting dinner. It had the same intended effects as alcohol, after all, inducing an unprecedented high.

Toby filled a glass with red wine.

Trish asked, "How long have you been a preacher?"

"Well,"—he handed her the glass and kept a glass of water for himself— "I've been preaching since I was ten. That photo there is me at fourteen, performing the Hands-on-Hands ceremony. It's basically an oath. Then I went and got my B.A. in English, M.S. in Theology, and Ph.D. in Philosophy."

"So, you're a doctor? That's impressive," she lied, bored by the conversation.

"Well, I always loved it, so why not study it?"

"I bet your family is proud of you."

"Yeah, I—"

His phone buzzed. Toby pulled it from his jeans pocket, looked at the screen, then rolled his eyes. Ignoring it, he shoved it back. "I do what I can," he said. "What about you?"

She raised a brow. Men rarely cared to ask such a thing. Especially if they had her alone; there was no need for the pointless banter. "Oh, I'm a secretary."

"Oh, what kind? I mean, where do you work?"

"At a car dealership. Um, I just answer phones and make appointments. Nothing too extravagant."

"That's—"

His phone buzzed again.

Toby huffed. "Excuse me…" He answered the phone. "What, Barbie?" he hissed as he backed away and stepped inside a room between the kitchen and the dining room. Trish guessed it was the bathroom. He whispered sharply into his phone.

"I can't—

"Don't—

"How?" he said, unaware Trish could hear him. Unaware that Trish could hear most things.

What if it's his wife? she thought. A young, handsome guy like that would be married to his college sweetheart by now. Trish searched the walls, not finding any dustless squares from missing picture frames. There were no pictures of a young, solo woman. Aside from modern photos of Toby, most of the pictures were tan with age, showing people wearing bell bottoms or dresses. Or religious cloaks.

Toby opened the bathroom door, shoving his phone in his front pocket again. Trish met him in the kitchen, abandoning her search.

"Is everything okay?"

"Yeah, it's my cousin. She's…troubled. She's always getting herself in a pinch and expects me to bend over backward to get her out. But I told her enough is enough; I can't keep bailing her out. I don't have anything else to give her."

"Should I go?"

"No, no, no. She's not coming over tonight."

"Are you sure?" The last thing Trish wanted was a surprise visit from a relative.

Trish looked at the clock. *9:19 p.m.* She groaned to herself. There was simply not enough time. Nor was there sufficient time to go back to the crowded campus and find another mortal with blood as fresh and rare as Toby's. It was too good to be true and too good to let go.

"I told her I'd call the police if she shows up," he said. "The only way she'd get in is if she breaks in. I took her key away and changed the codes a few weeks ago."

"Okay," Trish said frankly.

He smiled. "As a matter of fact…" Toby pulled his phone from his pocket and held the screen up to face her. The volume decreased from vibrate to mute. "She won't be interrupting us again."

Trish's mouth moistened. *Oh, dear, sweet Toby.* She loved it when they worked *with* her. It took everything not to pounce on him right then.

No. Not yet, Trish warned herself. She imagined the mess she'd make with him, mercifully sucking him dry—not wanting to waste time worrying about the chaos. *The tub*, she thought. If she got him to the tub before things got too difficult, the drain could do some of the work for her.

"Was that a full bathroom? I'm sorry to be nosey, but this house is beautiful."

He snickered and headed for the couch. He sat down. "Thanks. Yeah—" Toby pointed to the room he had just exited. "There's a full bathroom there, one upstairs, and a half-bath in the basement."

"That's cool." She followed him into the living room while Toby fiddled with his phone. Trish stood still, watching him. "Where's the music?"

"Coming right up."

He played an old R&B song from the '70s—she never kept up with that type of music because it changed so rapidly and too often. Toby set his phone on the coffee table next to his portable speaker.

"You like this type of music?" he asked.

No. "Are you kidding? Who doesn't like old school?" Trish swayed her hips and reached high, biting her lip and moving her body to the running bass guitar riffs underneath a carefully orchestrated brass quartet.

"I'm glad," he said, watching her.

"You know what would really make me happy?"

"What's that?"

"You dancing with me," she said.

"Yeah?" Toby rose from his seat.

His scent hypnotized, nearly making her dizzy. A savory, juicy pack hurling her way.

"Yeah," she replied. "Come dance with me."

Trish's personal buffet swaggered toward her embrace. Toby put his open palms on her waist. She wrapped her arms around his neck and buried her nose there, falling into his delectable scent.

"You *are* cold."

"Told you," she said, feeling herself warm under his touch. Then she felt nothing again. She only inhaled.

"Should I turn the heat up?"

"No. Just keep me warm."

His breath tickled her ear, and he turned his head to kiss her cheek. Even his breath awakened some new sensations deep within her.

Her heart raced, anticipation rocking her core.

Finally. Trish flicked her tongue up his earlobe and sucked air between her clenching teeth. She moaned softly.

Toby ran his hand up the small of her back and kissed her neck.

Her gums tingled harshly, her fangs extending to their full length. Her nails morphed into elongated claws, making her fingertips twinge. A thin crimson sheet coated her view of the TV: *9:31 p.m.*

Trish raised each hand to the sides of his neck, held on softly, and sank her tongue into his mouth, planting her lips firmly on his. Eager to taste him. Ready to bite into his flesh.

He moaned and clung to her waist, pressing her pelvis to his.

As they kissed deeply, she wrapped her hands around his neck and pressed hard on his Adam's apple.

CHAPTER 21

Feast

Toby planted his hands against Trish's chest and shoved. He even kneed at her thighs and hips.

"Get off—" he strained, choking on the end of his words.

Trish raised her elbows and brought them down on his shoulders, using her upper body to keep him still. She pressed his neck hard, watching his face turn purple. He gasped for air.

Human bones were so fragile; she could snap them with a simple squeeze. Trish had done it a few times before, when the catch got too belligerent. But Toby wasn't too tall; she overpowered him easily.

His heartbeat wildly as Trish stopped short of crushing his neck and killing him altogether.

Toby's efforts slowed, and he went limp under her hold. His wet, bloodshot eyes peered hopelessly, and deep, rapid gasps escaped his lips. The purple in his face grew deeper, and he became quiet. Finally, his weak blows stopped altogether, and his tongue slowly seeped past his lips.

His heart slowed, beating softly against her hands. Trish lightened her grasp on his neck. His legs buckled and his eyes closed. But she held him upright, using a quarter of her natural strength to keep him on his feet.

Trish removed her hands from his throat and hugged tight. His neck was warm and close. Veins thrust hard against his skin, taunting her, begging to be broken. She answered with stride. Trish sunk her fangs deep into his jugular, sloppily squirting blood. She ignored the mess for the moment and greedily indulged.

His sweet goodness flowed, covering her tongue, enlivening her flesh as she drank. She moaned. Energy from his life liquid made her awake, filling her with jolts of much-needed and much-missed vitality.

Like drinking pure, cold water flowing from a river after hours of play and dehydration... She felt her strength return, and her heart quickened. The aches that had plagued her for months slowly dissipated.

Mmmm, yes, she thought. Trish pressed her fangs harder against him, wanting to drain him...but not too quickly. It'd be a matter of minutes before he bled out.

She slithered and hissed at the cascade pouring down her throat. Enticed, she moaned again. If only he were bottomless... If only she could learn to trust him enough for manipulation, like she'd done to Victor Cross, her *forever feeder*. Her feeding was a fetish for Victor, but sustenance for her. The fling lasted for several years before, as always, a great thing had to end. If only Toby was more like Victor... If only Toby wasn't a God-fearing man who would turn her in. She couldn't leave him alive like she'd done with Victor. No. This was Toby's last stop. And for that, Trish savored the rarity. She appreciated the prize.

Her mouth bathed in a bloody, warm spring. Its heat and thickness made her quaver. Sweet convulsions tore through her, filling her mouth with so much blood, it fell out and ran down her chin. She felt the drops leave her face and suspected they'd met the floor.

Messy, she thought. *And he's going cold.* But she wasn't done with Toby's blood. She had to be quick.

Trish pulled her mouth from the wound and licked his neck before using her hand as a tourniquet. She watched for a second. Her hand failed to hold back the blood soaking it red.

She wrapped her other arm around his body and dragged him to the bathroom.

Shit, she thought. The red mess grew, with blood on the walls and floor, on her dress and boots.

Trish used her foot to slide the shower curtain and set his dying body inside the tub, but she realized she needed more time for cleaning than she had anticipated. It wasn't one she could leave behind with the many witnesses who'd seen them together. Sure, she had no DNA, and her face was that of someone much younger than her age when she was wearing the ring. The police would never find her. But still, she cleaned up her messes the best she could because anything could bring the law to her door.

Trish twisted the faucet knob and plugged the drain, allowing hot water to fill the space around his legs. As it flowed, she leaned over and lapped up the fresh blood spilling from his neck. But the sips felt more like a filthy tease. She needed...*wanted*...more blood swimming down her throat and filling her belly. Trish shut the faucet off, then studied Toby.

His chest rose and fell as his heart struggled to compensate for the missing liters of blood. *He is going to die soon*, she ruminated. This would likely be the last drink for a long time.

The risk of any interruptions was low. He didn't scream, so the houses around them were none the wiser, and she bet his friends didn't expect him back at the bar for a while. She had Toby all to herself and would make the best of a beautiful situation.

Trish pulled his shirt off and tossed it aside. She took one elongated claw and drove it deep into his left pec. Blood poured fast from his chest and hit her face. Toby expelled a soft, shallow breath before his chest deflated for the last time.

Trish pressed her lips against the new opening and sucked up the remaining blood.

When his blood clumped, she knew it was nearing the end. Trish left that small amount to add to the bloodied bath and looked into Toby's face. His lips were blue as ice, and his skin was as pale as the walls.

She immersed her lips underneath the hot bath and slurped: a fitting chaser.

Drunk, her vision went blurry, then clear. Her limbs prickled, and her body relaxed. She wouldn't mind drowning in Toby's life nectar; it'd be heaven. Trish had done many things out of the ordinary that night. She had gone home with a God-fearing professor who had spiritual paraphernalia on his walls, shelves, and around his neck. He was a man who lived alone but had many friends and family.

It was well worth it, just to taste it. Blood with the sweetness of honey and saltiness of buttered bread. I'm full again. I can focus again, she reasoned.

It had to have been about 9:45, and she needed to be home by midnight. As much as she wanted to stay, Trish knew she had to clean the scene, wash up, use Toby's car to dump his body at the construction site, then find somewhere to lose the car... *Or bring it back here,* she thought. Sometimes, it was fun giving the cops a real mystery to solve.

But his blood dragged her deeper into its depths. She wanted to lick the tub clean.

Five more minutes, she thought.

A faint beep sounded underneath the soft music.

Trish stopped, glaring over her shoulder at the living room, just past the bathroom door.

The front door opened, and someone let themselves into Toby's house.

CHAPTER 22

Barbie and the Gents

Trish sprang from her spot next to the tub, almost falling off her feet, full and dazed. It'd take a little bit to regain her wits after such a clean meal. Toby's blood made her higher than normal. It was the cleanest she'd had in almost a century.

Trish closed the bathroom door and locked it, and her claws and fangs remained elongated, on the defense.

"Toby?" a woman yelled from the living room, the music depleting to silence. "I let myself in! You can't *ban* me from Grandpa's house no matter how much this family likes to pretend that I don't exist."

Fuck, fuck, fuck, Trish thought, scrambling, searching around, seeing double at every turn. The only way out was through a window in the shower. But the window was Darwin's size. There were no closets. Only a sink, tub, toilet, a few decorations—none of which could be used as a weapon—and a basket…something else she couldn't fit in. Trish erred on the side of silence and hoped the woman would go somewhere else in the house, giving Trish the opportunity to dash out the front door.

She waited, listening to her heavy breaths and begging for focus as her vision played tricks on her, doubling every object around her. There were two faucets, two shower heads, and two bloodied pale Tobys. She wanted to scream.

116

"Toby? I know you're here. Just give me the jewelry, and I'll be on my way. You don't have to make this hard." Her voice sounded scrappy. Rough and grating.

The girl's scent made Trish gag as the air was consumed by chemicals and body odor.

She's getting close, Trish thought, eyeing the rod holding the shower curtain. A muted growl. It was plastic. *Useless!*

The girl huffed. "Toby!" she yelled. "That shit is rightfully mine! Grandpa left it *to me*! You have no right to keep it from me! If you don't want to cough it up, fine. But you'd better come out here and face me, coward!"

Silence.

"Come out here and talk to me, you—" The female stopped. "What the— Is that— Toby? Are you bleeding?"

Trish tightened her lips and dropped her head. There was no way the girl would leave, and surely, she might call the police. *Think, think, think!*

Trish held her breath in her throat. Her hands shook, and her jaw went numb. Her consciousness threatened to go dim, and she desperately searched for somewhere, anywhere, to hide.

There were no options.

"Wha—What the—? Toby?" The woman banged on the bathroom door. "Are you bleeding? Toby, answer me!"

She continued to beat on the door, and Trish heard the woman's phone beep as it called someone.

"What up?" a deep voice answered over the speaker phone.

"Get in here! I think Toby's hurt," the female shouted. "Open the door, Toby!" She jostled the doorknob.

The man sighed. "Man, Barbie, I *told* you not to get all trigger-happy on that Jesus freak. He don't—"

"I didn't do it, dumbass! There's blood on the floor and walls… and…he's bleeding. Get in here and help me, now," Barbie snapped, smacking the door with something hard.

Barbie, the troubled cousin who didn't call the police but demanded reinforcements. Trish shuddered.

"Toby!" she shouted, shaking the doorknob. "Open the damn door." She sobbed. "Toby!"

As more people poured into the space on the other side of the bathroom door, Trish stepped into the tub, knowing they'd breach any moment.

And there was nowhere to go.

So, she switched to the weakened offensive. Careful not to trip over Toby, Trish stepped into the crimson water near the drain and stood in the small gap between Toby's feet. She drew the curtain and balled her fists. Her focus wavered and her knees shook. She wasn't ready to fight. She was too weak to escape. Her body needed time to digest and readjust after feeding.

It's fine, she thought, blowing slow, shaky breaths. Trish shook her head, hoping to knock the dizzy, laxed spell. But she failed. The tub blurred, then cleared.

You can take them, she thought. *You will get out of here, even if that means—*

After a few kicks, the door imploded. Trish's throat tightened and her nostrils widened. The people reeked of cat piss and rotten eggs.

Meth, she thought. Someone's blood stream was riddled with the junk. They may have even had it on their person. *No wonder they didn't call the cops.*

Trish raised her fists, ready to fight. Or so she hoped. As she stood in Toby's bloody bath, blinded by hyped-up surprise guests, full to the gills with the best thing she'd eaten in a long time, she had some doubts on her readiness.

But she'd take them. Full or no. High or no. Cornered or no.

"Oh my— Toby!" Barbie shrieked. Her small silhouette bowed to survey the blood on the floor. Alongside her were two people. One was a thin man, the other husky and built like a truck. Through the translucent shower curtain, Trish could barely make out facial features.

Trish watched Barbie follow the gory trail to the shower. She brought her horrid stench closer with her advance.

Trish breathed slowly, ready to use her claws and fangs to fight her way out.

Barbie pulled the curtain back, but before Trish could slash her way out, she stopped and dropped her fists. The cold welcome was unforeseen but pointed her square in the face. Trish glared at the two barrels, ready to go off any second.

Bullets hurt, landing her in a coma once. Thankfully, Albert had been there to save her, but there was no doctor around to stop these people. There was no telling what ten bullets or so would do to her. Fixated by the possibility of her bullet-riddled death, Trish couldn't think of words or actions underneath the miasma that clouded her judgment. She went light on her feet, and fuzz con-sumed her thoughts.

The horrid smell intensified, and the stringy-haired, meth-rid-dled Barbie slammed the butt of her Glock into the bridge of Trish's nose.

CHAPTER 23

Blood

Trish groaned and sucked air between her teeth. Pangs raged in her face, and the dry blood in her nose made it hard to breathe. But she was sure of one thing: she was lying on her back, not in the tub anymore.

Caught in the depths of pain, she regretted the predicament. Her head felt like a truck had smashed into it, and her belly felt swollen and full. The aches in her face intensified, making any small movement cause sensory overload.

She had been gluttonous and hadn't allowed her food to digest. Now, her body worked against her. Trish struggled to remember how and why.

But then she remembered.

She could still smell him, could smell his sweet, sultry, delicious blood. Trish had drunk it—almost all of it. And he had died the moment she plunged her claw into his heart.

But then someone showed up.

Not only had it been an unnaturally long two months of starvation, but she'd also risked a lot for Toby, and for that, she was regretful because it might have cost her everything. But with that revelation, she smiled, basking in the aftermath of the best meal she'd had in decades. Toby's freshness took her back to the first time she'd tasted blood.

Trish trekked through the Virginian Appalachian wilderness, starved and confused about what she had become after the beast had bitten her just a couple of weeks prior. She'd made the decision not to return home because she felt a change deep in her bones: she wasn't human anymore. She was a monster, like the thing that had bitten her in the coop. For weeks, she walked on an empty stomach and unwillingly ignored the fact that she couldn't feel the chilly fall air on her face or arms. She only felt the sun that blistered anywhere it found skin. She walked aimlessly through the woods, sobbing and looking over her shoulder for people, mountain lions, and bears. She was sure that the blood on her collar and on her neck would call something nefarious out of its hiding spot. But nothing came. Only the sun scared her off into caves whenever the sky turned from black to dark blue.

Her body was tired as she limped along, looking for nothing and ignoring her new need. But it only took two weeks to give into the new urge while trying to eat plants, berries, and bark. None of the plant matter sat well with her body, which forced her to spit it back up. Trish had even gotten lucky by catching an opossum. She tackled it while it played dead on her approach. She used a makeshift spear to tear off as much fur as she could. Then she pierced the meat with her new fangs and chewed hungrily. The gamy meat seemed to hit the mark until she swallowed it. She vomited, leaving herself with an empty stomach and a sickening realization: she didn't enjoy the meat, but she loved the blood.

Only then did she give in to the metallic savory scent that beckoned her. Weakened and on shaken limbs, she followed the smell for miles until she stumbled upon the source—a wolf watching her the same way that she had been watching it. It growled at her, baring its teeth. She scolded and stepped slowly. It was time to give in to that strange new thirst she had. Trish needed something filling and sweet. Savory and thick. Blood. Her hungry dreams and leaking fangs demanded it. And the lone gray wolf was going to give it to her.

She had a strong hold on the spear that she'd fashioned for the opossum, wild animals, or humans who had threatened to kill her, and if she could use it on the sun, she would have. But no, it had a new purpose at that moment. It was for the wolf's neck. It was for the wolf's blood.

Trudging haphazardly through mounds of wet earth, Trish approached the wolf. It snarled and hunched, warning her. She crouched and stepped lightly over the crunching leaves. Balancing on her toes, she stopped a few feet away and watched it more.

It didn't move as it watched her back.

Then she stepped closer, gaining ground.

The wolf leapt and so did she. Trish threw her body into the animal, tackling it to the ground and dropping her spear in the process. As they rolled along the forest floor, her body snagged at stones, sticks, and tattered earth. The damage accrued left her with deep scratches, bruises, and bites as the wolf sank its teeth into her flesh and tore it free from her arm.

Both she and the wolf were covered in her blood. But she didn't let up, not with her teeth leaking venom down her throat. Not with her tongue and belly begging for the animal's blood. The new sensation had overpowered the pain, and she wrapped her arms around the wolf's middle. It clawed and nipped at her arms and chin, desperate to break free. Its teeth grabbed hold of her arm and tore more skin away.

She screamed, going hoarse as the unspeakable torment ripped through her body. Trish was sure her arm would never be repaired, but she didn't let go. She squeezed the animal harder. Once she had a fine grip on the wolf with her arms, and once they stopped rolling and she landed on her back, Trish crossed her legs over the animal's front, pinning it against her body. She grabbed the wolf's maw, plastered it shut, and planted her other hand onto the back of the wolf's head. Through the excruciating spasm shooting through her torn arm, she twisted the wolf's head. An abrupt pop echoed through the forest, and the wolf went still. Dead.

After the battle, she sat upright and plunged her fangs into the wolf's neck. Trish felt feral, not knowing how she managed the strength to beat a top predator. But her gums prickled, beckoning her to drain the kill dry. She complied, loving the animal's tang and ignoring the dirt and clumps of fur trapped in her mouth and between her teeth.

She let up when the blood clotted, giving a bitter taste. But she was full, bloated, and light-headed. Trish could've burst.

That day, she solved part of the mystery behind the monster she had become: blood was good, and human food was bad.

The rule, however, did not apply to her pregnancy. As Darwin invaded her mind, Trish came back to her current situation. It was no longer November 1889. It was November 2024. Alarm raised in her chest. *Barbie...* she thought, lightly jostling her arms and legs, which resisted her small movements. Trish maneuvered her wrists however she could. They rubbed against metal chains and a metal rod. She shifted her waist and was able to move a bit more.

Her heart slammed hard against her chest, and her eyes parted, welcoming the blurry light. It stung and beat at her intensifying head-ache. Trish twitched at her arms and legs but couldn't feel her toes or fingers. Her legs were spread apart, and her ankles were chained to the footboard. The chains around her ankle were so tight that she could feel them through her boots. She tugged and grunted, and then, finally, she opened her eyes fully.

Trish leered at the poor bastard leaning over her as he and the long barrel he aimed in her face came into focus. She blinked, hoping to adjust her eyes to the soon-to-be *very* dead man's face.

"Don't move," he snarled between gapped teeth, his short blond buzz cut golden in the light. A look of fear and seriousness crossed his eyes. He clenched his jaw while sweat dripped down the sides of his face. Nervously, he adjusted his hold on the shotgun and held his stance like an experienced hunter would, ready to blow her skull wide open.

He called out, "Barbie, she's up!"

CHAPTER 24

Chained Up

Barbie—a short, pale, bony girl half the gunman's size—burst through the door. She took a spot next to the blond. Her red, puffy eyes glared wildly at Trish.

"Did she talk to you?" She peered down at Trish. "Do you talk?" she yelled.

Trish was too busy trying not to vomit to respond. The man smelled bad, but the girl was rancid.

"Nah, she didn't say shit," he said. "She just opened her eyes, and I called you in, just like you said to do." A hint of irritation lingered on the edge of his words.

Barbie went on yelling as if Trish were hard of hearing...or thinking. "Why is Toby's blood on your face?"

Drowsy and full, Trish struggled to gather the situation—it was best not to respond.

"You *deaf?*"

Trish held the woman's eyes. Barbie scowled hard underneath years of serious drug addiction. Craters and wrinkles riddled her round cheeks, making her appear decades older than she was. Her blood reeked of urea and floor cleaner, and her skin smelled like cigarette smoke. Trish felt her full belly turn.

"Barbie." Another man came into the room, worry etched across his face. He looked young and could've been a student at Miller. "Hey, he's calling again."

"Okay?" she asked, rolling her eyes.

"W-well, what should I do?"

"Goddamn it, Tay, don't fucking answer it! I'll call him in a second. I'm dealing with *this* right now." Barbie turned to Trish. "I gotta find something out before I call him back."

"Like?"

Barbie huffed. "Why does that matter? Get out and keep watch. I don't want Steve showing up with me not knowing he's here."

"He knows where—"

"Go watch!" she growled.

Tay tugged at his waistband, adjusting his sagging pants against his hips. He huffed. "Man, aight."

Barbie shook her head. "Idiot," she mumbled.

The blond snickered, tightening his finger against the trigger.

"Right, Danny? I mean, that fucker ain't listenin' when I tell him to go and do something, and this dumb bitch is acting like she can't hear me." Barbie peered back at Trish. "*Hello,* why did you kill my cousin?"

Danny guffawed.

"Did Steve put you up to this?" Barbie growled.

Who the hell is Steve? Trish thought.

Barbie was small, but damn it, did she have a mouth. A nasty one at that. Even physically, Trish could see the rotting rows of teeth in the girl's mouth. They were all the same color too, corroded by drugs and smoke. Barbie's lips should never peel back to reveal such a tormented maw. With little information and no plan, Trish waited, needing to know more about her captors. Sometimes, allowing humans to talk allowed plans to formulate themselves.

Barbie looked down, flashing a murky smile. "So, you're not talking, huh?" she asked.

Trish gazed at the ceiling, dreaming of ripping the girl in half and draining her blood into the toilet where it belonged. Her stomach curled and twisted, threatening to let go of a meal she worked so hard to get. She had waited months for it, only to end up drowning in the collective stench of druggies. The scent of the meth addict was strong and foul. Even on Trish's most desperate of hunts, she avoided them. It was kind of like how Darwin avoided carrots and peas. He'd spit them out and throw the bowl across the room. In fact, he seemed to be doing that with most of his food lately.

Trish's heart lurched. She had no idea what time it was, but she knew it was time to leave, and her exit needed to be swift. She fixated on the two people who were making that almost impossible, presenting a challenge she didn't need or want when she still had a body to dispose of, along with three others who needed dealing with. Or at least three that she *knew* of. There was no telling how many new people were within the house, and it was hard to figure anything out with Danny's shotgun waving around.

A belligerent swipe crossed Trish's cheek, shoving a flash before her eyes and into her thoughts. Her cheek stung after Barbie's bony fingers slammed into it. Her speed was almost impressive. With all the poison in her veins, Trish thought Barbie would be as sluggish as she. But no.

"Hey!" Barbie shouted. She slapped Trish again. "Answer me!"

Trish clenched the metal chains in her palms, slowly working them, weakening the links and waiting for the perfect time to snap them. But she had to take care—the shotgun could go off and rip her face to bits. She could withstand many things, but she couldn't defeat bullets at point-blank range. The past had taught her that.

Trish slowed her movements.

"Still deaf?" Barbie asked.

Trish said nothing.

Barbie cocked her head, and with a sly quickness, she slammed her fist against Trish's nose, right where she'd pistol-whipped her upon their first meeting. Whiplashed, Trish blinked frenetically. A pulsating cramp rippled through her face. The crushed cartilage took another blow, and Trish stopped breathing for a few seconds.

Powerful little bitch, she thought. Rage willed her to get her hands on Barbie, crack her open, and let her bleed dry. The police would have fun trying to figure out how it all happened.

Blood ran down Trish's cheeks, and she pulled in deep breaths, swallowing the blood falling to the back of her throat. She jostled her feet and arms, stressing the chains. Trish stopped, then wiggled her nose, knowing it was busted. The crushing pain begged her to stop trying to disturb the pulverized gristle. The room spun as she breathed slowly through her mouth. She wasn't as high from her meal anymore, putting her an hour out from the time she ate Toby. But the new assault amplified her off-kilter focus.

Barbie flung her fingers, trying to shake away the pain. She winced, then closed her hand and pressed her fists to her sides. "Do you know what you just did to us? Huh? *Answer me!*" Barbie's pale face turned purple with anger and tears. She turned back to Danny and said, "What are we going to do?"

"We can't just look for valuables around here? I know your cousin got"—Danny stopped and cleared his throat—"*had* some shit around here. I mean—"

He stopped talking when Barbie gave him a dismayed look and avoided her response by staring deeply into Trish's eyes. Trish wondered what color he saw. She was angry and defensive enough for her irises to be red. But she was full, so they might've been pink.

"He hid everything that was left, smart ass," Barbie said. "If I knew, I wouldn't bother with asking him for shit in the first place. I would've cleared this place out years ago! But that's why we're here." She scoffed. "It took *nothing* to convince Toby to give me a few dollars once I got ahold of him. But that's never going to happen again, thanks to this *thing*! You should just fucking shoot her." She pulled at her shoulder-length blonde hair, then grunted.

"Family. What good are they?" Danny asked Trish.

Trish's family meant everything to her: Darwin because he was her son, and Randel because he was her son's father.

Toby, however, didn't seem to mean much to Barbie.

CHAPTER 25

Junk

Ugh, Trish thought as she watched Barbie bite her thumbnail. Once it detached, she spit it off to the side. Barbie and Danny had spent the last several minutes bouncing ideas around; none of them made any sense. Their thoughts ranged from robbing the nearby neighbors to trading electronics with Steve that weren't worth a damn at a modern pawn shop.

Trish had grown more bored than angry during her time in the drugged-out think tank. She breathed in small remnants of Toby's scent hiding underneath his foul cousin's. His smell reminded Trish of how she had ended up there. She pulled her wrists and ankles whenever Danny looked at Barbie for answers. With them in the room, progress toward weakening the links was slow, but ongoing. She had broken zinc-plated steel chains with her own strength before, but it wasn't a quick process; she needed time away from Barbie and Danny to speed it up. The thought of Mel again rushed to the forefront of Trish's mind. This time, she saw Mel cackling while she watched her new friend—and Trish's replacement—Tucker slug Trish in the face. His small curly afro and thick sideburns dripped with sweat, and his open silk shirt was wet with her blood. They'd taken their time wrapping her midsection with the chain, locking her in a wooden chair. Her captivity was made possible because Mel spiked Trish's water with PCP. Once the ordeal was said and done, Trish realized that her so-called best friend put her into a coma that lasted for over a day and a half. During that time, Mel made the mistake of pulling the ring off Trish's finger, waking her up. When Trish came to, Mel stood behind Tucker, berating Trish and asking, "What the fuck are you, huh?" She pulled her fiery hair back into a ponytail, something Trish had never seen her do in the nine years that she had known the woman. She also knew why Mel's skintight bellbottom pockets were so stuffed; her ring was in there along with other things.

Trish squeezed her eyes shut and forced herself back to the present.

Mel is dead, and you might be too if you don't get out of here, she griped to herself.

"Are you at least in his will?" Danny asked, raising his thin, golden eyebrow.

Barbie sighed. "What a stupid quest— He probably doesn't have one. He's only thirty."

Thirty-three, to be exact.

"Well, are you sure he's dead?"

Barbie glanced over her shoulder. Also curious, Trish lifted her head to see what Barbie had been looking at. Just at the base of the TV stand was a bloodied white sheet covering a motionless lump the length and size of a man. Trish knew what they'd hidden underneath the sheet. Toby. *Tastebud-teasing Toby*. Her gums itched, and her mouth recalled the tasty blood that had flooded her tongue.

Though full, she could make room for more of the rare drink.

But she had bigger problems, all of which were caused *by* that rare treat.

"You tell me," Barbie said to Danny. "Is he dead, Danny?"

Danny didn't say a word. He only watched Trish with a very familiar sensual glint in his eyes, exploring more than just her face. She watched him ogle her breasts and thighs underneath her bloody dress. He had a clear line of vision between her spread legs.

"Well, what are we gonna give Steve?" Danny asked. "He's probably on his way over."

"You think I don't know that?" Barbie said. She covered her face with her hands and grumbled something too low for Trish to understand.

Then Barbie peered one of those dark, deranged eyes at Trish.

"We'll give him her," Barbie declared. "I was going to kill her because of that—" She pointed to Toby's body. "But no, we're going to give him…her. We'll give him her. If he sent her here to do this, then we can give him her: trade her for a pardon. But if he actually *didn't* send her to do that—" she nodded in Toby's direction— "and it turns out that this is just a crazy bitch, then we can still give her to him for a pardon." Barbie dropped her hands and smiled big, as if it were the best idea she'd ever had.

"He's pimpin' now?" Danny asked. This time, he looked over at Barbie.

Trish stretched her legs a little, feeling the chains tighten against the outsides of her ankles.

"No. But look around, asshole. You see what she did to Toby?"

"Well, yeah, I mean—"

Barbie walked up to the head of the bed and stood next to Trish's face. She inched her index finger toward Trish's upper lip. Then she stopped and, scowling at Trish, said, "If you bite me, he will pull the trigger. You hear me?"

Trish stared.

Barbie lifted Trish's upper lip, exposing a fang. "See that?" She ran a fingertip down Trish's tooth. Then, with her free hand, she pulled her phone from her pocket and aimed the backside at Trish. It made a clattering sound as if snapping photos.

Trish rolled her eyes. Her fangs were still extended because she was trapped in predator mode. Her anatomy told on her, working against her. It was something else she couldn't fully understand. But she let them go on.

Barbie smiled a rancid grin. "Fangs," she announced. "Real too. They did that." She pointed at Toby's body. "I saw them when we moved her from the tub; her mouth fell open." She leaned a little toward Toby. "At first, I was so mad that I wanted to outright kill her. But—and I just thought about it—Steve is into this kind of shit. He—"

"Barbie, he was high when he said that stuff," Danny said, snickering. "You didn't think he was serious, did you?"

"I know that, but let me finish. He said he knew a bitch that had fangs and paraded around like a—"

"Vampire? I know. I heard him say it too. I was there. And I also know that he was high off his ass when he said it."

"Stop cutting me off!" Barbie demanded. "He would want her. He would… Shit. I'm thinking this *is* her. This is the thing he was talking about! Don't you see? That bastard sent her here." She turned giddy, smiling hard and almost bouncing on her haunches. "We're in the clear."

Barbie snapped another picture of Trish. The blinding white flash brought about what seemed like millions of black specks that coated Trish's vision.

"Barbie, you talkin' crazy. Vampires ain't real," Danny said. "Her fangs are fake. She paid somebody to put them in… Those claws she had on were fake too… There are a lot of people into weird shit, and I'm sorry to say, but Toby mighta been into that kinky blood stuff. It just went too far. She's a person, Barbie—a *weird-ass* woman."

"Yeah, well, we'll let Steve be the judge of that, assuming he doesn't know her already."

"Okay. So, what are we goin' to do about Toby? You know the cops are goin' to assume we did this, 'specially because you just *had* to move him, gettin' our fingerprints all on him and shit."

"I couldn't just leave him there." Barbie paused for a minute. "And I'm still thinking on that."

Danny huffed.

"What's more important right now is that we get Steve to take her. Shit, it'll clear all of our debt," she said.

Barbie lifted Trish's lip and flicked at her fang. She snickered when Trish flinched.

"See that?" Barbie asked Danny, amused at Trish's response. "Does it hurt? Huh?" She flicked at Trish's tooth again. This time, Danny laughed along with her. "Not so big now, *vampire*."

Trish clenched her jaw, her heart slamming into her chest.

As soon as that gun is gone, she thought. *As soon as that damn gun is—*

"*Oh*, she don't like that," Danny said.

131

"What? Being called a *vampire*?" Barbie asked. "Huh? That's what you are, right? Right?" She leaned in close to Trish's ear, suffocating her with that heavy metal and chemical stench. "I hope Steve dissects you and sells you to the cops, ounce by ounce."

The girl stood up and went back to thumping, popping, and flicking Trish's fang with her middle finger. The pungent odor of ammonia and vinegar harassed Trish's nostrils. With dead patience, Trish nipped like a dog and broke skin. Her face crumbled when a little of Barbie's blood cursed her right fang. The blood tasted like an old penny that had been drowned in industrial cleaning supplies.

Barbie yanked her hand back to her chest, and Danny slammed the barrel down, bursting Trish's lips. She wailed, tasting her own bitter blood trailing down her throat. Trish panted through her pained lips. She filled her cheeks with bloody air and pushed it through a shaken face.

Trish could tear the room apart, starting with the dickhead waving the shotgun around. But blowing a fuse might get her killed. If she jumped on Danny, Barbie would attack, giving Danny the chance to shoot, and that simply wasn't an option. No shooting. The last thing Trish wanted was the neighbors—or worse, the police—skulking around. She also didn't want a bullet in her own ass.

Shit. The situation wasn't ideal. *Sloppy and greedy*, she said to herself, resisting the urge to think back to the bar. Toby could have slid away when he had the chance. She should've cut him loose and headed to a party to find easier prey. Now, she had at least four bodies to get rid of.

Barbie cradled her hand. "She bit me!"

"Yeah, she's a biter, all right," Danny said, correcting his stance. "And if she bites Steve, you'll probably have to answer for it. He's gonna wanna see her teeth—"

"If he hasn't already seen them. If she isn't the one he was talking about."

Danny sighed. "Right. But before we hand her over, Barbie, whether she's a freak parading around like a vampire or not, he's gonna wanna see."

"She can't bite through metal," Barbie said. She looked down at Trish. "Can you?"

Trish huffed, wondering when the girl would catch a clue. She had nothing to say to Barbie, and the sooner Danny lowered the gun, the sooner Trish could get out of there.

But she'd have to take them one at a time.

"Oh, you don't want to answer my question?" Barbie said. "I'm sick of your shit. Hang on. I got something for you." Barbie trudged for the door. "Oh, wait until you see what I got for you! Biting-ass bitch," she yelled, heading for the hallway.

CHAPTER 26

Ol' Blue Eyes

Danny looked Trish up and down with a sliver of pleasure shining through his hard gaze every now and again. When he finally acknowledged her eyes, his seemingly blank expression lifted into a smile.

"You're in trouble now," he teased.

Trish raised a brow.

His eyes lit up. "Y—" He cocked his head. "You understood me?"

She smiled.

"So, you're not deaf?"

Trish shook her head slowly.

"Hm. Why not answer when Barbie asked—"

"Because I don't want to talk to her," Trish said. "I want to talk to you, the level-headed of the two."

He chuckled. "Yeah. Barbie's far from the one that *anyone* wanna to talk to." Danny's eyes softened and became welcoming. Yet his stance remained stern, and he continued aiming at her face.

"So why—" Trish started, but stopped when feet pounded the steps.

Barbie made her way back into the room. This time, she had something in her hands: Trish's leather purse. She dug through it. Her eyes widened, and her brow dropped menacingly.

Sweat formed on Trish's brow, and desperation tugged at her gut. *I need this fucking gun out of my—*

"Might want to keep this, huh?" Barbie pulled out the wallet and opened it. She held up the Visa card, then put it in her pocket and looked down at the license. "*Hm.* You don't look as old as you do on your license, *Patricia Weston.* But you *do* look an awful lot like this little fella here." She pulled out a picture of Darwin—the one with him sitting on a small oak chair and smiling, showing off his gums. She managed to get his hair to form a swoop over his forehead. His toasted almond skin was prominent in the glow of the flashy sun-shine backdrop. "Maybe I should go to that address on your license and see if he's there. I always wanted baby-skin shoes."

They laughed.

Barbie slid the license in her pocket and tossed the wallet on the floor. Trish's need to murder the people in the room intensified.

But she waited.

"Old-ass phone," Barbie said as she tossed Trish's cell phone on the floor. She continued pawing around. "Keys to a car I don't need and—oh. What's this?"

Barbie pulled the ring from the center pocket. She lifted it and eyed it in the light after tossing the purse over her shoulder. It hit the wall, throwing most of its contents out onto the floor, and landed near Toby's grave.

Barbie eyeballed the ring, her eyes glowing at the fat diamond. Then she looked at Trish with disdain. "Eh. It's a little dated for my taste, but the jewel might be worth something. What is that? A diamond?" She slid it onto her bony finger and put her hand out in front of her face, studying. Her lips twisted, then she smiled. "Nah... I think I'll keep it. You won't be needing it where you're going." Barbie turned to Danny. "Watch her. I'm going to get Steve over here so we can get this done and over with."

"Well, what about Toby?" Danny asked again. "We can't just leave him here."

Barbie went quiet for a minute. "We'll call the police as we're leaving and tell them the truth: We found him like that, and the person who had done it was already gone."

Danny smirked and shrugged. "Works for me."

Not for me, Trish thought. *Not good for me at all.*

***

Danny stood there big and cocky, his buzz cut moistening. His shoulders quavered, and his breath hastened.

He was getting tired of holding the gun.

Trish smirked. It had been about twenty minutes since Barbie left the room. He'd give in soon enough.

Danny hadn't tried speaking with Trish again, even though it seemed like he wanted to. He adjusted his shoulders and licked his chapped lips every now and again. It was almost like he enjoyed watching her watch him.

But the staring game wore on Trish's dwindling patience. They only watched and listened to each other breathe. She was sure he secretly wished he could have his perverted way with her. Trish, however, envisioned breaking his neck and getting her ring back from his friend. She drew weary with every second, and her gut swarmed with uncertainty. No. The night couldn't end like *that.* She needed to get back home, and she needed to be out of there before more people showed up. The chance of that happening drew closer to impossible, but she had to do *something.* She watched her captor, reasoning with his flirting eyes. Whatever went on in his head might be a fantasy not too far off from their very reality. She could give him that, or at least help him believe she'd give him that. Trish's heart swelled as her mind conceived a plan.

Trish smiled big, acknowledging his wishes, ready to undo his imagination instead of losing her own temper and risking her life.

Possibly, she reminded herself.

Danny lifted a brow, curious about her smile, she assumed, because his tight lips lifted in one corner, smirking at her.

"Is she your boss?" Trish asked. Nasally, she cleared her throat, freeing the drying blood from her windpipe.

Danny smacked his teeth. "No, she's my *colleague.*"

"Oh," Trish said, chuckling. It hurt her face to laugh, so she grimaced.

He frowned. "What's so funny?"

"Nothing. Nothing. I just"—she cleared her throat again—"didn't know that friends treated each other that way."

He groaned. "She's not my friend. And treat each other like what?"

"You know…the way bosses treat their bumbling lackeys. She treats you like shit—like she runs the show and you take orders. You respond to her a lot like a weak, emasculated man would."

Danny scuffed. "I don't give a fuck about what you think."

"That's fine. I only asked because I'm not okay with being the submissive," she whispered. "But I figured you would be though." She moaned and ran her tongue over her lips, tasting her own blood, full of old iron and fresh plasma. "I love it when men give in to domination—someone who gets high off reducing themselves to nothing before embracing the challenge of rebuilding. That's what *real* men do." Trish arched her back a little and rolled her hips. Then she lay still, holding Danny's wandering eyes in her own.

"I believe that," he said. "With your thick bones—you might look thin, but you're heavy," he said. "You could probably pick a man up by his neck. You probably…you probably crack a whip, shred a fucker up until he yells the safe word."

Checkmate. She silently praised his naivety. "You like those games, huh?"

He smiled. "Yeah. Can't find too many chicks 'round here that play it right though."

"You wanna play with me? I promise I'll change your mind about the girls around here."

Danny's smile faded. "What? So I can end up like that sorry bastard under the sheet over there? No, thanks."

"Oh, come on. That…that was purely accidental. Toby and I were playing, and it just got a little too rough. He wanted me to suck his blood—that's how he got off, ya know? It's *always* been the *only* way to get him off. I swear. I even stopped and told him that he could die, but Toby was a fiend, forcing me to keep going. He always wanted me to keep going. Flirting with death was his high. And who am I to tell a client no? I mean—we've done this before and…and…" She summoned fake tears. "So, I did what he said. And when I noticed he was dead, I *freaked*. Okay? I was…I was so afraid. I didn't know what to do."

"So, what happened to his chest? You did that too, right?"

She paused for a second, sulking. "I was trying to save him."

"So you're a doctor now?" Danny's face went stern.

Trish didn't respond, only wished she'd fashioned a better lie. The hole in Toby's chest didn't scream *accident*. It screamed *murder*. Quick to backpedal, she changed the story by altering the perspective.

"You don't understand. I panicked, okay? I tried to make it look like something else… I—I wish I could undo everything. I just—I just want to go home. I'll do anything to get out of here. I… But I understand why you won't let me go. Barbie would kill you."

"Barbie ain't my boss!" he snapped.

"Then let me go. Please? I'll do anything. Just, please…"

He raised a brow and looked her over. Stubbornness and disobedience overtook his need to please their crack pipe queen. Danny had a point to prove; Trish could tell.

"Anything, huh?"

She nodded desperately.

Danny studied her closely, standing silent, leaving Trish to grow anxious. Then, after what felt like minutes, his face crumbled, and he shook his head. "Nah. You're all bloody and beat up. Nah… Hell no."

"I promise I won't bite. I just want to get out of here. This is so *fucked* up. I fucked up." She fell to tears. "Oh my God, what have I done?" She turned, laying her cheek onto the wet puddle. "I just wanna go home. Please, let me go home?"

Danny sighed. "Look, stop crying. All right?" He lowered the barrel but kept his finger on the trigger. "You'll do anything if I let you go?"

"Yes, if you promise to let me go. I'll leave right out the window. Barbie wouldn't even know we did anything. She wouldn't even know that you let me go without her permission."

His nostrils flared, and he raised the barrel again. "That bitch *ain't* my boss!"

"All the more reason for you to let me go. Steve sounds like he's Barbie's problem. Not yours. You let me go, she can't do anything about Steve. He'll take care of her."

Danny snorted. "You talk about Steve like you know him…"

"You're right. I don't, and I don't want to know him. But you guys sound *really* afraid of him."

"I'm not scared of nobody. That's *Barbie* who's scared of him."

"Why?"

Silence.

"You can at least tell me where she's sending me, if you don't plan on—"

"Barbie is afraid of Steve because he gets all weird and crazy, on some mad scientist shit."

Trish furrowed her brow.

Danny went on. "He uses people that don't pay him, or people he just plain doesn't like, as guinea pigs for shit he mixes up in his shed. Some sick-ass drug concoctions. Like Super Speed and Jumpy Meth. His shit messes people up. The sicko even performs weirdo procedures on people that have bad reactions to his stuff. Only a real psycho can do that to people, and he gets away with it because his uncle owns the police around here. Steve is a nut job with too much money and too many friends in the police department." Danny's face twisted in disgust. "I mean, this guy cuts off body parts and dumps them in different chemicals as a way to determine if those *chemicals* are good candidates for his new drugs."

Great: stupid, rich, and crazy, Trish thought, imagining what Steve would do to her, a monster. He was so elusive that she couldn't imagine him with a human face. Instead, she envisioned a man wearing a rubber apron and a plague doctor's mask.

"Most times, people don't even know that they're test subjects. He'd just sell some messed-up stuff, and if they die, it's called an overdose. For him, it's easy for tox reports to go missing or get marked over. Steve *owns* Miller, so he can do whatever he wants. I just know that I don't take or buy *shit* from him. I get my stuff from a guy in another county because I'm not stupid."

"Does Barbie owe Steve? Is that why she—"

"Hell yeah, she owes him. He gave her some stuff to push in the trailer parks around the county because everyone knows Barbie as the Trailer Park Queen. But her dumb ass went on a hiatus and smoked or shot up most of it. She won't tell us how much, but I'm sure it was thousands of dollars' worth. She might've given it away to her short-term buddies over in Detroit before she realized they did most of the drugs while they partied for weeks and didn't pay for shit. Who knows with her? It's not the first time she's done somethin' like that. I keep tellin' her not to smoke Steve's stuff, but she don't listen." He cut his eyes. "Anyway, she thought the preacher would bail her out again, but…" Danny paused for a second, his face going a little pale. "Like I said, I wouldn't want to owe Steve a nickel. He will kill you and maybe use you for some weirdo shit. The guy is from a different *planet.*"

"Oh. So he'll kill me anyway?" Trish asked with a lump in her throat, hoping to escape before Steve showed up, if he wasn't already downstairs. It wasn't that she was afraid of him killing her—she was sure she could take him. But people, namely the police and his clients, would look for Steve if he went missing.

"Yeah. Probably. But since you got teeth like that, he might do something else with you. He swears he's seen another vampire running around, and claims he *has* one but won't show it to anyone." He snickered. "It's weird because he only talks about it when everyone is nice and high."

Trish stopped the fake tears and rose to all seriousness. "Another vampire?" she asked. *Victoria Scott?* But Trish didn't ask for names. In fact, she regretted her initial response.

"Well, yeah, but I don't believe that shit for a second. But he does, probably from all those experimental drugs he does. He experiments on others, but he tests a lot of things on himself. I'm sure he thinks there's an imaginary vampire in his basement. Probably a sick dog or something. Anyway, he might turn you over to the FBI, or something like that, if he doesn't dissect you on the spot. I think it's all crazy really."

"No. It's not." Trish had been a monster so long that she forgot what it was like to be a human discovering one. She had met a monster the day she died, and that night didn't end so well for the beast. Trish avoided capture for that very reason, becoming a social pariah before being torn apart and examined for traits and characteristics that could help humans. She didn't want to be a source of research for *them*, her food.

"Hm," Danny said. "Nah, I think it's all bullshit."

Disbelief festered, and she spun into a whirlwind of confusion. Here was a pile of evidence proving things like her existed alongside humans, but still…

"Vampires ain't real. You're just a pretty girl that's a little messed up in the head," he grunted. "You're out here running around, biting people, eating blood and shit." Danny paused. "A pretty girl like you can get away with that, and I have to admit, I can see why some people find it hot. But you're just one of those chicks that get plastic surgery just to look like their favorite *something*."

He gawked at her breasts then looked back into her eyes. Danny grinned, changing his mind on a recent criticism. "I'd let you do it too. I'd let you drink me dry. All the way, until you were full. I'd die a happy man if you did that right after I let you suck my cock." He grabbed at his lap. "No teeth, of course… Well, maybe a little."

"Really?" Trish asked.

"Yup."

She tilted her head at the request. Trish was repulsed, wanting to vomit at the mere suggestion. She would trade him for roadkill off the side of the road any day; it smelled better. But instead, she shifted her eyes down to his bulge.

"And then you'll let me go?" she questioned.

"Yeah," Danny said. "Can't have you melting away in the morning, right?" He chuckled. She didn't. "But I was kidding about sucking my blood. I don't do that shit."

"Heard," she said softly.

"I'll let you sneak out the window, just like we agreed. That sound like fun to you?"

Trish nodded.

"But you gotta promise not to do me like that poor fucker over there."

"I promise."

"This isn't a trick, is it?"

Trish sighed. "Of course not. I want to get out of here."

"Well then. Let's do it."

Danny rested the gun on the floor, just on the other side of the footboard.

CHAPTER 27

Window

Danny planted his knees on either side of Trish's bound body. Pressing her hips between his curled legs, he made his way up her length, his hardened crotch bulging through his once-baggy acid-washed jeans. When his knees reached her shoulders, he loosened his belt and presented the vile thing. It pointed at her as it drew closer to her chin.

Trish licked her lips and lifted her head as much as her chained wrists would allow.

Danny groaned. "Hurry up, before Barbie comes back," he demanded.

"Okay," Trish whispered. The tip of his flesh was nearly touching her nose.

Quickly, Trish pulled her head back and jutted it forward, slamming her forehead into Danny's groin. His hard dick met the aggressive thrust. Trish only wished the headbutt had been harder. If it had, he would've passed out.

Danny yelped and tensed, holding himself. "Bitch!" he blurted, struggling to breathe through his clasped teeth. He fell over, landing on the mattress, frozen in pain.

Trish yanked and pulled her arms and legs, willing the chains to give. Intense bouncing and the chiming of chains brought on a lot of noise—so much so that Trish grunted and shouted, "Come on!"

The gun slid down from its spot against the footboard and onto the floor.

Slowly, Danny scrambled. Thick veins erupted across his strained face, and tears rose to the wells of his now bloodshot eyes. Although limber, he rolled onto his back, moving for the edge of the bed, possibly fighting to reach for the gun.

But Trish's right arm broke free, splitting the metal chains holding her, bending them into something useless. She balled her fist and smashed it into his left temple.

Danny cried and grabbed her fist before it could come down hard again.

Come on, she thought, continuing to kick and bounce. Trish pulled her arm away from his grip as she yanked at the bondage holding her other extremities. Her hand free from his grip, she punched his wet left eye.

His head thrust back, and more chains gave, freeing her left ankle and left hand.

Terror-stricken underneath his bloodied face, Danny rushed for the end of the bed, wildly reaching for the gun.

With her now free hands, Trish grabbed the nape of his neck and pulled him toward her, still attempting to break her other leg free. "Pervert," she snarled.

Danny jerked but failed to detach. He shouted in pain.

The final tug of her right leg broke the remaining chains. Trish wrapped an arm around his chest and covered his mouth with her other hand to stop his yelling. She pressed her lips against his ear and whispered loud enough for him to hear over his pained grumbling. "*Shhh, shh, shh.*"

He balled his fists, trying to swing, eager to fight. But she was too strong—she was *always* too strong. Trish wrapped her legs about his wide waist.

"Thank you, Danny," she said. "I'll make this fast…for the both of us." With a hand still over his mouth, she used her other hand to grab the back of his thick neck and clutched hard.

He kicked, cried, and screamed underneath Trish's suffocating hold. She twisted his neck, cracking every bone and demolishing his trachea.

Danny gasped before going quiet and still. He went limp in her lap. She dropped his neck and watched his body fall over on its side. Trish pulled her legs from around him, and blood rushed from his mouth, soaking the sheets.

Trish got to her feet, fighting the onslaught of pain beating on her face. The subtle dizziness also served as an important reminder: she was still a little high, still full.

Maybe it wasn't as late as she thought.

Yet still, she didn't know the time. To confirm, she dug through Danny's pockets, finding his phone and a few lost cigarettes. There was even a ball of what smelled like cocaine. She tossed the cigarettes and drugs on the bed with him and hit the power button on the side of his phone. Trish was met with a locked screen—on it, a photo of a naked blonde on her knees in front of an American flag backdrop.

11:48.

Trish tossed his phone on the bed and searched the floor around her. Her eyeliner and lipstick were near Toby's corpse, closer to the TV stand. Her purse was at Toby's feet, and her foundation, phone, and keys sat next to the shotgun, just underneath the foot of the bed. The wallet was also close to the footboard.

She scooped everything up and stuffed them inside her purse before snatching up the shotgun and aiming at the door. The bottom of her palm wavered over Danny's name, which was ingrained into the wooden stock, and her index finger flirted with the trigger. Trish envisioned how easy it could all be…wiping them out with a single shot to the head as she stepped silently throughout the house—a much-deserved ending to such a horrific night.

She took in a deep breath and lowered the gun. She pulled the bolt back and dumped the housed shells out onto the floor. Four golden shells: more than enough for the two people left that she knew of. She stuck her finger inside, and didn't feel any more.

No one needed them, not even herself. All she needed was her hands and stealth.

The gun blasts would increase the number of dead bodies from four to unknown because the neighbors would hear the commotion and call the police, sending more witnesses.

No. Trish didn't need the gun, and neither did the two downstairs. She sighed. She was sure the others had guns, and they'd pull the trigger in a heartbeat, dragging the police over to Toby's to find Trish either bleeding to death or dead.

And if Barbie were clever, she could get away with killing Trish. Barbie could tell the cops that the dead, or dying, woman was a threat, since Trish had been found standing in a tub of blood along with Toby's bloody corpse. They'd believe Barbie and seek immediate justice if Trish was still alive to face it. The town of Miller would erupt in sadness, asking their God why Toby, their beloved preacher, was brutally murdered by one of Satan's demons. Although Trish had no relation to Satan, those people were too nose-deep in the Bible to realize or believe any different. The authorities would kill her for science, or to prove God's existence once and for all.

Stupid, she thought, glaring at the back of the bedroom door and pondering over an easier way out that didn't seem to exist. Trish looked down at the gun and decided the risk wasn't worth it. She'd have to be quiet; she had to be smart, and she had to be fast. Trish headed for the closet just behind the bedroom door and opened it. She set the gun inside, just next to her purse. She removed her boots, which were soaked through with Toby's bloody bath, and also set them next to the purse.

No need for them to hear me coming, she thought. She even removed her socks and stuck them in her purse.

Trish listened and heard footsteps below, pacing back and forth. She heard the chilly quiet night on the other side of the window, which sat opposite the room door. Trish wished she could disappear into the darkness and leave Barbie to explain what had happened to Toby.

But Trish needed her ring. Or better yet, the serum inside it, and leaving evidence of her existence behind, such as her credit card, license, Darwin's picture, and her coat wasn't an option either.

She recoiled.

The thought of Barbie wearing her prized possession made her quake. Trish imagined tearing Barbie's finger off, snatching the ring, and then shoving the dead finger down her nicotine-stained throat.

No matter how she killed Barbie, a few things were clear: Trish needed her things, she needed to kill Barbie and Tay, and she needed to get out of there soon.

"Danny!" Tay shouted, his throat trembling.

To Trish, that only meant one thing: he had heard the commotion.

"D-Danny?"

Trish held her hiding spot in front of the closet door. Once he opened the bedroom door, she'd be behind it.

I guess you're dying next, she thought.

Trish braced herself as the door opened, hiding from the unsuspecting man.

CHAPTER 28

Slippery Fingers

"Danny," Tay called out as he pushed the door open.

Tay probably expected to find Trish helpless and tied down like a prized mythical monster, too afraid to make a move on the scary man with a gun. No shots went off, so she couldn't've gotten out.

Right?

She smiled at his bewilderment when he faced the truth.

Tay came to an abrupt stop and stared at the man on the bed.

Danny was slumped over, his chest and cheek against the bed. Blood seeped from his mouth; his twisted neck lay limp. His lips were separated, as if he had something to say, but the words remained in his last thoughts. Redness spilled from between Danny's jaws and covered his tongue which stuck out past his crimson teeth. One wide, startled blue eye stared, while the other was closed and bruised, plumped purple. Dark blood coated the side of his face and his once blond hair sopped up the redness from the sheets.

"D-D-Danny?" Tay asked, approaching gradually, visibly shaken. "Danny? Danny, man...are you...?" He reached out and touched Danny with a pointed finger, then drew his hand back. Tay gasped. "Shit!" he spat. "Danny...Danny!"

Trish watched him drown in disbelief as she waited for the right time to pounce.

Tay advanced toward the footboard and picked up whatever was left of the chains. Then he peered at the four angles of Trish's former prison. He backed away from the bed, unknowingly getting closer to the door where Trish was hiding.

Just a few more steps, she thought, readying herself to reach out and grab him.

But he moved forward, straight for the headboard. "Bitch…" he mumbled to himself, peering at the window. His shoulders dropped, and he relaxed a little, possibly due to a false sense of safety.

Yeah, there was a window, and yes, she could've easily left that insane night behind. But that wasn't her intention. She wanted her stuff back. So, no, Trish hadn't dipped out the window; she was in that very room, ready to break his neck the same way she'd broken Danny's.

Tay threw a frantic glance around the room. "Where's the gun?" he asked, going up to the footboard and dropping to his knees, *clearly* not finding it underneath the bed.

The element of surprise wouldn't work on Mr. Curious. That opportunity was long gone. Time only sank deeper into the night, and Trish had to get going.

As Tay got to his feet, Trish pushed the room door, closing it fully. The soft click grabbed Tay's full attention. His mahogany skin paled, and he glared wildly at her.

"Oh, *hell* no!" he shouted, backing up and moving alongside the bed. Eyes wide and breath bursting from his chest, Tay shouted, "Barbie! Help! She got out!"

Trish rushed toward him, and he searched around in a frenzy, looking for a way out. Before he could find it, Trish reached, aiming to snatch him up by his neck or even his hoodie—whatever she got ahold of first. But he dropped onto the bed and crawled over Danny's body. Trish scratched the air, her fingers missing him. Tay's feet met the floor with a hard *thump* when he landed on the side of the bed closest to the window. He rushed toward the footboard, ready to round the bed and bolt for the door.

In his haste, Tay's foot caught onto the bloodied sheets covering the corpse on the floor, partially revealing Toby's crimson neck and face. Tay stumbled and belly-flopped against the floor with an enormous *clunk*.

Trish went for him, her raven hair wisping on quick winds. She moved briskly, baring her teeth. The fight had gotten old.

But Tay was fast.

He maneuvered, turning on his back. He bent his knees and forced his boots into her belly.

The kick knocked the wind out of Trish, sending her body flipping over the footboard and bouncing onto the mattress. Her body twisted, and her forehead came down over the edge of the bed, slamming into the nightstand surface with a large *thunk*. The pointed edge shoved a dizzying flash before her eyes, and she fell onto the floor, face-down.

"Ah!" she growled, as pain concentrated on her face. Fresh blood trickled down her forehead, and catastrophic aches took her head. Trish considered running after Tay, who had just gotten the door open. She listened to his shouting as he stumbled down the steps, warning his leader the monster had gotten loose, and that Danny was dead.

Trish took time picking herself up from the floor. She thought, and she thought hard. She thought about how difficult the rest of the night was going to be. She pondered ways to clean everything up. Trish even thought about how fast she had to make everything happen. She considered the gun in the closet. It'd be loud, but it'd be fast.

She wondered why Tay hadn't killed her with *his* gun. Not only did he find his partner dead, but he was also confronted by a monster personally. Clearly petrified, Tay should've pulled a weapon and fired in a heartbeat.

So why didn't he?

Then it hit her.

He doesn't have a gun, she thought. *If he had one, he would've used it.* Through the disruptive vertigo and the onslaught of a nearly debilitating headache, she finally found her footing. Trish headed for the dresser and found a clean white t-shirt. She wiped the new blood from her face and formed a plan.

Stealth, she thought. *They can't know I'm down there.* Then, and only then, would she find Tay first and then neutralize Barbie, assuming they were the only two left. That fact, Trish still wasn't sure of.

CHAPTER 29

Stay

Trish winced and wiped a trickle of blood from her forehead. The bleeding had slowed substantially, but she felt an achy bruise forming at the source. She huffed and walked over to the door, stopped short at the opening, and crouched.

The hallway light was still out, which was a plus. She didn't have to worry about anyone getting a good peek of her there. Trish peered around the corner.

Tay's feet pounded throughout the first floor of the house, and he called out for Barbie, shouting about how *dead* Danny was and how *deadly* Trish was.

Trish huffed. They were on alert now, something that'd make sneaking up on them almost impossible. As the night went on, it only seemed to get harder to end it, keeping her stuck in the same place. She could've been walking in circles.

Trish was better off fleeing into the night through the window. She'd done it before, leaping from the top floor and landing on her feet when the front door was no longer an option.

But leaving the ring behind *wasn't* an option. And neither was leaving her son's picture, her license, or her jacket, which was on the couch downstairs; it could possibly tie her to *the mess*. She shuddered as she stalked the hallway. The scene was grisly, and it was only going to get worse. *The police don't need a reason to show up to my door.*

Trish stopped at the top of the steps and listened for her chance. All she heard was Tay shouting for Barbie as he stomped around. Trish glanced at the foot of the steps, which was polished in the living room's glow—she'd be easily caught there.

Mm. She'd have to head down once he left the room or stepped outside. *Damn open floor plan,* she thought.

"Barbie, where are you?" Tay shouted. "Barbie! She got out!"

The sliding door off the kitchen opened and closed.

"Shhh. You want the neighbors to hear you?" Barbie asked. A menthol-stained breeze followed her inside. "You gotta—"

"There's no way I'm staying here. She's gonna kill us!" Tay said. "She's gonna— Oh my God—" He struggled to breathe and speak all at once. His hysterical outburst shuddered with unease.

"Dude, what are you talking about?"

"S-she killed Danny, and we're next. I don't wanna die like that!" A short pause. "We gotta get out of here. We gotta—"

Barbie shushed him again. "Slow down, Tay," she said with a faux calmness. "Now, what the fuck are you talking about? Where's Danny?"

"Danny...D-Danny's dead and the bitch is out. She's out, and she killed him. She-she snapped... His neck was all twisted. I don't...I—"

But Danny deserved it, Trish thought.

"She killed Danny?" Her voice rose with curiosity. "Why didn't you shoot—"

"She killed Danny!" he shouted as if Barbie were hard of hearing. "He had a fucking shotgun in her face! How did she kill him?"

"All right, all right, *calm down.*"

"Don't tell me to calm down! She's not scared of guns, Barbie. Can you even kill a vampire by shooting it?"

"Tay, calm down."

"No! Fuck you! I'm-I'm out. I'm—"

Trish heard him stomping for the door, just opposite the staircase.

"Wait!" Barbie said. Quickened footsteps followed him.

"Let me go!" he shouted, and they shuffled a little. "Let me go! I'm not doing this shit! I didn't—"

"Shut up!" Barbie spat. "Listen, no one is going anywhere."

"I'm leaving," he hissed.

"No, you're not. You're going to stay right the fuck here and stop that thing from escaping," Barbie snarled. "You wanna know why you're going to stay here and help me?"

He didn't respond.

"Because if she kills me, then that only leaves you. And if you're the only one still alive, you're the only one left responsible for paying the debt to Steve. And you know how he gets when people owe him, right?"

"I don't owe him nothing! You do!"

She sighed. "Tay, you know that don't matter to him."

"This is bullshit! You not draggin me into your shit, Barbie! I told you not to—"

A cynical chuckle. "That doesn't matter. What does matter is how your parents will feel when they find out what you been up to. They think you're working some third-shift factory job while you study *all day*. But that's not true, Tay. You sell coke, pills, and heroine for me, and *we* sell them for Steve. But if I'm dead, and Steve finds you alive, you'll end up in pieces at the bottom of the river. You don't want that to happen, do you? Because I sure don't."

Foul bitch, Trish thought as she listened to Tay's breathing. She almost felt bad for him. But he was in the wrong place at the wrong time. He had to die just as much as Barbie did.

"You a hateful bitch," he muttered.

She giggled. "Oh, I know. But it's all right because I won't let anything happen to you," Barbie said. "You'll get your money for this semester and the last two years of school if you help me wrangle her for Steve. No more jobs after this."

A thoughtful pause.

"Yeah, a'ight. After this, I'm out. Don't call me. Don't look for me."

Their voices descended as they left the living room and headed back toward the kitchen. Trish listened, hearing remnants of Tay's resignation, but they were far enough for Trish to make a move.

Taking the chance, Trish crept down the stairs, sure to press her back against the wall once she hit the bottom step. She peered around the corner.

They stood in the kitchen, just on the other side of the island and out of view.

"How am I supposed to get the bitch? She can kill me, just like she killed Danny," Tay regurgitated.

"And I said she isn't going to," Barbie snarled. "Do you see her down here now? Because I don't. She's still upstairs, if she didn't jump out a window yet. You better hope she's not gone. Go get her tied down and wait for Steve. He's close by, and he hates waiting."

"Can you at least help me? And maybe he can help too?"

"No! Go do what the hell I said, Tay! You're really wearing on my damn—"

"Danny is dead! Did you hear me say that? He's dead! How is that when he had a gun? I'm not dealing with that crazy bitch by myself. But you can. Be my guest!"

"So, you *don't* want the money for the semester? Is that what you're saying?" Barbie asked. "You want to go back home and tell your family that you failed, saying goodbye to being—"

"Stop hanging that over my head!" he snapped.

She breathed deep. "You will go find her and get her ready for Steve. Then you will be off the hook. That's the last time I'm saying it…"

Trish planted her feet against the hardwood floor. She crouched and crept along the wall across from the staircase and into the living room, then inched over toward the L-shaped couch, trying to catch them in her view. But she hid behind the closest armchair, needing to stay out of *their* view.

They moved closer to the sliding door. If Trish peered around the armchair, she would see them. *Another plus*, she thought.

"Now, go tie her up," Barbie went on. "I'll be outside, waiting for Steve. Your gun loaded?"

154

"No! You said we were only coming over here to your cousin's house, not being attacked by a vampire! I didn't even *bring* a gun!"

"Stupid, you're never supposed to leave home without your gu— I don't have time for this. Here…"

Trish peered past the chair and watched Barbie give Tay a handgun she had concealed between her bony hip and the waist of her jeans.

"If she does anything stupid, graze her."

"If she lunges at me again, I'm killing her," he said. "She's not breaking *my* neck. No. No way." He cocked the pistol.

Barbie headed for the patio door and disappeared outside.

PART 6

Monster

CHAPTER 30

Death of a Monster

As Trish hid behind Toby's armchair, she couldn't help but shake at the knees, growing anxious for her escape and ready to confront the current threats before another showed up. She contemplated taking Tay down right then. He hadn't moved from his position in the kitchen, just in front of the patio door. He hadn't even stepped foot toward the staircase or the living room. He aimed Barbie's pistol into the living room, frazzled enough to let out exasperated, shaken breaths. Trish was sure he'd miss if he decided to fire.

If *he's not a pro,* she thought. Trish pulled her hand down her face. There were too many options with too many unknowns, and too many unknowns led to unsettling uncertainties. But there she was again, dealing with a terrified human with a weapon. They were unpredictable when they were in that state. She'd seen them do horrific things in the name of self-defense many times, starting with the monster who'd bitten her.

***

After she pulled herself up from the bloody floor of her family's chicken coop, Trish followed the sounds of the mob for miles as they carried the captured beast deeper into the West Virginian wilderness. Their obscenities were so loud, she could have been within the group herself. They gleefully demanded things like "Die, beast!" or "Burn it!" and "Send it back to hell!"

She stopped short of the group and hid within the shadows of the trees, but she stayed close enough to capture the earthy aroma of burning hickory. It mixed with their collective whiskey breath, which was staggered with whiffs of roasted pig ears from the barking bloodhounds. Her stomach turned at the overwhelmingly malodorous scents.

Still, Trish contemplated drawing closer to the ruckus. She wanted to see the creature's wicked eyes one more time. Its bright pink irises burned in her memory as her body ached, trying to adjust and understand the recent attack as she exerted energy to run and watch.

The men hoisted the beast up on its feet. Its leathery face bled, and its bony malnourished arms and ribcage-imprinted chest were bare, open to the night and out for the prosecutors. Its belly bulged, protruding out, full of her blood.

She quavered and pressed her hand to the wound on her neck. The pain had subsided, but fear had not. Even though the monster was surrounded by men on all sides, she felt vulnerable to its danger. It was a thing of nightmares, a demon that touched her, fed on her... did something to her. She couldn't quite put her finger on it, but there was something different about her—a primal change that made her want to flee. Made her want to die. She felt it in her bones.

The men secured a noose on a high limb of an oak tree. The loop dangled about eight feet above the dark leafy ground. A burnt and bloodied mess, the monster hissed and cried as four men pinned it against the tree and one of them, Trish was sure it was Cutler because of his drunken swagger and hunched form, wrapped the loop around its neck. It took five men to pull the rope, which lifted the howling monster off the ground and hefted it into the air. Its rasping cries were overpowered by the remaining cheering men who either held onto one of the four bloodhounds or held onto one of the five torches. Its body swung violently as it kicked, its feet searching for something to stand on. But there was nothing.

She hated the monster, and she hated herself more for wanting to help it escape.

***

Trish's stomach flipped as her own fears intensified, and her hiding spot behind Toby's armchair seemed to shrink as time ticked on. If she jumped up, and Tay pulled the trigger, the neighbors could call the cops. If the police showed up, they'd turn her over to the government, who'd marvel at a true anomaly of nature by tearing her open and studying every element of her being. But if she waited for Steve to show up, he'd probably leave her alive long enough to watch his sickening torture firsthand, if there was any truth to what Danny had told her. If Steve showed up, she'd be outgunned and out of luck.

Then, what about Darwin? She was sure Randel would be all right, but Darwin didn't deserve to live without his mother. And what about the ring? It was more important than Trish herself—there was so much to learn about the serum which filled the inner walls.

Trish let out a muted growl and peered over her shoulder at the clock sitting on the fireplace. 12:35. Tay was petrified, and that might work out in Trish's favor. If she moved quickly, she could take him down.

But his nerves could force him to pull the trigger, she reminded herself.

He'll miss. She took a silent breath and considered the one thing that she had over Tay: he didn't know where Trish was, but she knew exactly where he was.

CHAPTER 31

Steps

Trish stood and pulled her weight off her haunches. She watched Tay go wide-eyed with surprise, then propelled herself, charging at top speed.

Tay desperately pulled the trigger. *Click. Click. Click,* the jammed barrel rang. "No!" He slapped the side of the pistol with his palm.

Trish dove and lodged her shoulder into his gut, forcing him back onto the piano. The instrument blurted a disjointed chord at the blow.

Tay grunted and dropped the gun. It clattered against the tile floor and slid. He tumbled onto the floor, just in front of the piano, and used his hands and knees to hold himself up, fighting to find his breath. His arms shook, and he coughed, dropping bloody spittle from his lips. Shortly after, he picked up one of his hands from the floor and held onto his midsection.

Trish was sure she'd torn one of his organs.

He hacked and coughed, sucking in wet and heavy breaths.

Trish picked up the pistol and disassembled it. "Where's Barbie?" she asked, tossing parts into the living room, kitchen sink, and behind the piano.

Tay continued coughing.

Trish watched him struggle. She was sure he'd spit up a lung from the way he stayed there on the floor, coughing and gasping.

She sighed. "You people made things overly complicated for me...but I'm willing to let you live if you tell me where Barbie is," she lied. She knew the girl was outside. But if he told her exactly where, Trish could plan accordingly.

He said nothing.

"Really? I'm offering to let you go in exchange for her, and you won't do it? You want to die for her?"

"Fuck you," he grumbled.

She sneered and marched for him. Then she reached, ready to end his suffering and move on to the last human in her way.

When Trish reached for the back of his neck, he lifted, standing on his knees. He carried what looked like a pocketknife upward and stabbed her in the abdomen, just shy of her right kidney.

Trish shrieked as more blood soaked the front of her once olive dress. The pain was almost blinding.

Surging with aches, Trish grabbed the handle and yanked. Wincing, she stopped. "Dammit!" she screamed.

Tay finally pushed himself to his feet. With Trish still hunched over, he tried to pass her. Though her middle had been torn with a knife stuck inside, she spun around and grabbed the hood of Tay's sweater, tightening it around his neck.

He yelped when she pulled him back, stopping him from reaching the sliding patio door.

"Barbie!" he yelled again, nearly falling backward.

Trish tightened her grip on his hood while bracing herself to pull the knife from her midsection. She grabbed onto the handle but stopped and looked at him.

No. The knife would have to wait. She couldn't risk him getting away. He'd have to die first.

Make it fast, she said to herself with gritting teeth.

"Barbie!" he yelled, summoning his partner. She was nowhere to be seen, and why would she want to bear witness? She only cared about her pardon. But Trish couldn't care less about Barbie's agenda. She only knew her own: kill Tay, kill Barbie, and get out of Miller undetected.

Trish pulled Tay toward her as she imagined herself detaching his head and pitching it at Barbie once she found her. But as Tay backpedaled, he swung his fist and hit the knife, jamming it deeper into Trish's flesh. She screamed, lifted him by his shirt, and threw him over the kitchen island. He slid across the surface and landed on the tile floor with a big *thud*.

Grimacing at the jarring pain, Trish yanked the handle, extracting the blade from her stomach. Blood gushed from the new wound and pooled onto the floor. She wailed.

Tay rounded the island and limped past her, headed for the sliding door again. Trish rushed for him, stifled by the new pain. She reached and missed when he ducked and headed the opposite way, changing course for the grand piano. Tay headed for the door on the other side and opened it.

Before he could close it, Trish leapt and crashed into him, sending them both down the steps, tumbling hard toward the basement. Tay cried out when a loud *crack* erupted as he slammed into the wall. Trish felt her own bones protest in agony. They smashed against each step on the way down. Both Trish and Tay hit the bottom floor hard, her landing on her shoulder, happy it didn't snap. Tay landed on top of her and scrambled to get off, maybe to find somewhere to hide. She pawed at the tile, desperate to get on her feet yet slipping on her own blood.

Before he could get far, Trish grabbed his ankle and crushed it with an angry clutch. He fell forward, landing on his belly. Finally on her feet, she limped and placed a heavy foot on his back, just over his heart.

"Where is she?" she hissed.

He didn't respond, only cried in pain.

She leaned into her planted foot, adding unfathomable weight to the boy's failing airway.

Tay screamed into the tile, blood seeping from his mouth. He was dying. Trish could feel his pulse racing as his blood pooled onto the floor.

She leaned in closer, ensuring he could hear the seriousness in her voice. Ensuring he could feel death coming *before* it arrived to take him. Wanting him to know he'd made the wrong decision by showing up to Toby's that night.

"Where...is...my *ring?*"

"I"—he coughed—"I—"

Convinced he couldn't move on his own or speak underneath her unbearable weight, Trish let up. "Tell me where my ring is."

"I-I—"

She huffed and leaned in, crushing his chest.

He groaned and cried out. "I'll...tell you..." He sobbed. "P-please...don't k-kill...me."

"Talk," she growled.

"B-Barbie has...has it." He spit out more blood, and his body convulsed.

"Where is she?" Trish spat.

"She's...waiting in the backyard for Steve..." he cried. "Just... just please, don't kill me!"

"*Shh, shh, shh,*" Trish said.

Watching the boy cry for his life didn't move her. He didn't have to show up with Barbie. Tay could've left. He didn't have to die that night. But—just like Barbie—Tay wasn't leaving Toby's house alive. Not only had he stabbed Trish, making it harder for her to escape, but he'd also seen her face.

Trish picked her foot up and slammed it against his back one, two, three times. His bones cracked, his back caved, and blood soaked the floor around him. Tay stopped shaking and moving; his heart seized.

Trish watched the red pond encompass her feet, painting them crimson.

One more to go.

CHAPTER 32

The Kitchen

Trish climbed the steps slowly, listening hard. She walked on her toes, cringing at every creak and small noise that erupted around her as she leaned in with every step upward. The tight staircase only got tighter. Invisible hands squeezed her lungs, suffocating her as violent spasms pulsated from her forehead down to the hole in her abdomen. But as she crept into the unknown, she tried to ignore her condition by focusing solely on the ring. Battered and beaten, the ring was the only thing that could fix her; she needed to go back to her human form. She imagined the euphoric conversion as serum pumped through her veins and arteries, mending all her wounds and ensuring another day in the sun. The ring was her lifeline, and she needed it back. Otherwise...

There is no otherwise, she thought.

As she ascended to the next floor, she didn't see feet standing in the dining room or kitchen.

No. The first floor looked clear. Barbie was still outside, which was good *and* bad. Good if Trish could hide and wait for Barbie to come inside, taking her by surprise.

Bad if she doesn't come back inside alone.

Trish stood at the top of the staircase, fully exposed. She couldn't hear much over the singing crickets just on the other side of the patio door, but she could smell everything. She smelled Tay's blood, which wasn't as dirty as Danny's, but there was still a small chemical stench.

166

She could smell Toby's clean, sweet blood, which only meant that the tub was still full of it. Trish's face twisted as she caught a whiff of Barbie. Her horrid stench spread around the first floor, so much so that pinpointing her exact location was impossible.

Heart slamming, Trish rushed over to the sliding door and peered out. The back yard didn't appear to be encased by a gate. It was as if Toby shared his yard with neighbors who lived several hundred feet away and the woods along the back end. The thick tree line blended with the night.

Trish smacked her teeth and looked over her shoulder at the clock in the living room.

12:58 a.m.

The night had grown later while her patience grew thinner.

Trish searched the living room for any sign of Barbie. She had to be close by. Trish looked behind the armchair and in front of the couch. She peered up the stairwell. Then she looked at the bathroom door. As she contemplated returning to the place where'd she'd been caught earlier, Trish rethought her position. Two intruders were down, and there was only one left: the unpredictable hot head.

Barbie would shoot to kill. She'd use her gun on Trish and pin all deaths on the vampire. *Barbie* would go down in history as a hero, the town's savior. Her sunken face would be plastered across every news outlet. She'd probably get a folklore, and everyone would remember her.

It pained Trish to think about what Randel and Darwin would think.

No. Trish turned and headed back toward the piano to watch the living room, hoping Barbie would appear there.

She's not a hero. Barbie will die a worthless, narcissistic, thieving addict, and I'm going to kill her. That was Trish's plan. That was her *only* plan.

The patio door slid open, and Trish spun around as Barbie let herself in. The woman wielded a shotgun and lifted it to aim, neglecting to close the door behind her.

Trish sprinted for the living room, leapt over the couch, rolled over the seat, and landed next to the coffee table.

Barbie let off a shot, which tore through the couch's back. Bits of wood cut through the air, and clumps of cotton and shreds of fabric floated about, raining down on Trish. She stayed on the floor, listening for movement through her ringing ears.

Trish lifted the coffee table and stationed herself between the legs, using the tabletop and couch for cover.

"Just give me my shit, and I'll leave!" Trish shouted, hoping the meth head had time to make a deal, one that would save her life... for all of five minutes.

"Oh, so she talks!" Barbie announced.

"Give me—"

"Where's Tay?" Barbie shouted.

Trish huffed.

"Oh, am I *inconveniencing* you? Am I getting in your way?" Barbie barked.

"Look, I just want to leave, okay?" Trish shouted. "I want to get out of here, just like you do!"

"No. No, no, no. You think you can just kill my friends and walk away? You think you can come into my cousin's house, kill him, then leave scot-free? No way, bitch!" Barbie pumped the barrel, sending spent shells clacking onto the tile floor.

She was still in the kitchen.

She looked around, finding Barbie aiming. Barbie stood in plain view of the open sliding door, and the ring on her finger glinted in the yellow light.

Certain that the table wouldn't survive the next blow, Trish abandoned her position and rushed for the staircase.

"You're not leaving, bitch! You owe me!" Barbie shouted.

Barbie shot again, and the shells snagged the edge of the wall, just as Trish had passed it.

"Ugh!" Barbie growled as she pumped the barrel again.

"Give me my *shit*, and I'll leave! You don't have to die like the others."

"Oh, okay. Sure. I'll take you up on your offer, right after I introduce you to someone who *really* wants to meet you! I'm sure Steve would *love* you."

"We could be gone by the time the police get here! I'm sure they're on their way with all the shooting you're doing," Trish warned, hoping Barbie had drugs on her. If she did, the last thing Barbie would want is for the police to show up. "You don't want to explain why you have a shotgun, do you?"

"If the police come, I can just put this on you. You *did* kill everyone."

"Just give me my ring—"

"You want your ring? Too fucking bad. It's mine now!" Barbie said.

"Barbie—"

"Don't say my name! You don't know me!"

"Okay, *dumbass*, I'll kill you and make it very painful if you don't put the gun down and give me the ring."

"Oh really?"

"Yes. Really. And you know I can make that happen. Both of your friends had guns, and I killed them," Trish growled.

Barbie giggled nervously. "I'll blow your head off first."

Trish sighed. "No, you won't."

"How could you be so sure?"

"Because what are you going to give Steve for the drugs you stole?"

A pause.

"Huh," Barbie said. "Come out and prove that I won't shoot you then."

Trish let out a pestered chuckle. "I'm sick of bickering. Just give me my things, and I will leave. Your choice: you can let me go and go gallivanting off to Kingdom Come before your psycho drug dealer finds you, or I'll kill you right here."

Quiet.

Baffled, Trish knew that what she wanted wasn't much, and if Barbie knew what was best for her, she'd comply.

"Are you there?" Trish asked.

Still quiet.

Then snickering, before Barbie's chuckling grew louder, morphing into a deranged cackle. Yes, the evening had been insane for

Trish, but, for a second—and only for a second—she'd imagined how crazy it must've been for Barbie.

As Barbie calmed down, she said, "You must think I'm stupid, just like everyone else. People always have something to say about what I'm doin'. But you wanna know what I tell them? Shut up before I kill you too. I've killed plenty, and I got receipts—marked graves all across I-96, bitch, and you better believe I'm not done. Nobody knows what's best for me. So, they all fall in line before I make them fall for good. I make the rules, and I run this shit—I've been doing it for *years,* vampire.

"Since I was fourteen, I knew my own dull-brained mom didn't know what was best for me as she sucked the tit of that shit church, waiting for her turn for some recognition. But they never gave it to her. She was the maid. She was the babysitter. But I'm for damn sure nobody's slave. I get my own money. I don't need this house or those holy robes to show me a damn thing.

"I'm different. I want everything, and I *get* everything, one way or the other, because I always make the final decision. I make the moves—I delegate. I make things happen." Her voice dipped. "And when things get in my way, I *remove* them. So, with that, here are the real options: you will die here, or you're going to come with me and die somewhere else."

"You actually think I'll allow anyone to take me anywhere?" Trish asked, almost amused. "You're mistaken. You're not getting your way *this* time."

"Try me," Barbie said calmly.

Trish paused for a second, deciding her counter—charge at Barbie because that shotgun was out of bullets. Yes. Trish believed Barbie had used them all. If Barbie had shells, she would have rounded the corner by now and shot to kill. But instead of calling attention to that very fact, Trish decided to wait a little longer. She humored the girl. "Where are you taking me?"

"I'm not taking you nowhere. Steve is coming to get you," she said. "But that idea about gallivanting doesn't sound so bad. I might turn you over to the police for a reward. If I had known that vampires were real, I would've spent my life hunting you and all your friends down. Including your little son," she said. "It would be like murder for fun, and everyone would thank me for it."

Trish cringed, disgusted at the woman's mention of Darwin at all. But then, she reminded herself of who she'd been talking to. *Ms. Lalaland*, Trish thought while rolling her eyes, but said, "I'd do the same thing."

"You *already* do the same thing…"

The women stayed quiet, with Trish not knowing what to say. She decided not to justify her restraint any longer.

"Look, I don't have time to deal with this," Trish said. "I just want to leave. I'm tired and it's late. And you and your friends have been a major pain in my ass. Give me my shit, and you will live."

"I'll live? Are you stupid? Or did you forget that I have a gun, and you don't?"

Trish huffed, and said, "You're out of bullets."

CHAPTER 33

The Barrel

Barbie remained quiet. She held her position in the kitchen, aiming the empty gun at the staircase. Time dragged on, and the pain in Trish's stomach pulsed. She breathed easy and slow, keeping herself centered and her mind on the task at hand.

For a second, Trish wondered what plan Barbie could conjure up outside of waiting for Steve. There couldn't have been another strategy; she'd been defeated. And Steve hadn't showed up yet. Trish was starting to believe that he wouldn't show up at all.

After a few minutes, Trish finally said, "Let's stop playing this game, and you give me my things so I can go."

Barbie huffed. "You think I'm going to let you walk out of here after what you did? The only way you're getting out of here right now is if you kill me."

"Oh, but I *am* leaving now," Trish said. "And no one will stand in the way of that. Now, you get one last chance before I come over there and break every bone in your body. Then I'll wring you out like a used washcloth right before I rip your finger from your hand and take my ring. I'll stroll right out the front door while you lie ragged on the kitchen floor. The police will find your rotting corpse frothing in your rancid blood." Heart slamming and vision going red, Trish felt her claws extending through her cramping, trembling fingers. Her fangs leaked, dropping venom into her mouth and down her throat. She had a taste for blood, but not for drinking.

"Those threats don't scare me, lady," Barbie said softly. Then she sighed. "Is that all you want?" Her voice shook a little, fear exuding from her words.

Trish smirked. Barbie had come to her senses.

"Yes. I want my things, and I want to leave."

"All right," Barbie said. "Come get your stuff and get the fuck out of here."

"Take the ring off and put it on the counter." Trish peered around the corner, placing an eye on Barbie. Her straight face appeared docile. "Give me the ring, and I'll leave you alive."

Barbie clamped the gun tight between her side and elbow, freeing up her hands but not dropping the gun, the barrel aimed at the floor behind her.

"I want my son's picture and my license too," Trish demanded.

Barbie went to pull the ring from her thin finger. It slid off with ease. "Come on, vampire. Get your stuff. You can even have your credit card back." Barbie slammed the ring on the island. She pulled the picture, license, and credit card from her jeans pocket and set them next to the ring. "Come get it," Barbie barked, her sincerity fading into a scowl.

Clearly, Barbie hated losing, and deservingly so, Trish enjoyed every second of it. But she hid her own victorious grin and rushed through the living room. She watched Barbie with one eye and her things on the counter with the other.

"Hurry up, vampire. You might want to move a little faster than that because you won't be leaving once Steve gets here."

The title *vampire* made her gut fold, forcing a mild cringe.

Barbie snickered. "*Ah. Vampire.* You ashamed of what you are?"

Trish said nothing as she reached the counter, claws retracting as she made her way there.

"The least you can do is answer me," Barbie said.

"It is what it is." Trish picked up the ring and slid it on her fourth finger, left hand.

"Since this is all finally over, can you answer a question for me?"

"What?" Trish said sharply, picking up Darwin's photo and her—or Patricia Weston's—license and credit card. She slid them underneath her bra strap.

"Is your kid and his dad a vampire like you?"

"No."

"Oh, so I'm guessing they don't know what you are? A murdering bitch? They don't know that you go around killing people like Toby? Like Danny?" She paused. "Tay?"

Like I'm about to kill you. "No," Trish said, turning to Barbie, ready to crush her face.

"Maybe I can pay you a visit at 550 Fallon Lane and tell them who you are. I'll prove it to them too. I'll lure you outside into the sun and watch you sizzle and burn. We'd have a daytime bonfire. I'll teach your baby how to make s'mores."

"You're high."

"Mmm, yeah. Maybe a little."

"Hm. I'm not surprised. Toby told me you were troubled. I mean, you know how Toby *was*. So passive—that was his way of calling you a waste of time."

Barbie's smile faded. "He didn't say that. My cousin did everything for me," she said with a bit of spite between her teeth.

"Really? Didn't he lock you out and threaten to call the police if you and your meth trash friends showed up begging for money? I mean, that's what he told me."

Barbie narrowed her eyes. "You don't know shit about my family."

Trish smirked. "You know what? I took great joy in killing your buddies. Danny was a sexual deviant—he let me loose right after he told me about your reign as the trailer park queen. He said he was going to throw you under the bus when Steve showed up. He said, *I hope Steve dissects her like he does the other non-paying crackheads.*"

"He didn't say that." Barbie's nostrils flared.

"Did he? Tay tried leaving the house altogether when he saw I was free. He was going to leave you here alone with the monster that drank your cousin and killed one of your henchmen. Tay was literally bolting for the door. Remember? He told you he was leaving." Trish shook her head slowly. "That one lacked every bit of loyalty. That's probably why he had weak bones. It was so easy to crush his chest and back with my foot, even with a knife wound in my stomach. It was almost upsetting—anticlimactic really. But I guess it could've been from all the drugs too. He only dealt with you because of— well, you know why.

"But I guess that's why Steve doesn't trust you. He isn't coming, is he, Barbie? Doesn't he know to never have an addict sell his shit? I mean, that was your only job, and you failed. No wonder your family cast you out and decided to give Toby everything. The church, money for college..." Trish looked around. "This beautiful house. Hm. Maybe you're right. Maybe I shouldn't have taken him from you, because without him, you are nothing."

Barbie inhaled deep, raising her shoulders and putting on a small smile. She watched Trish move and talk.

Trish went on. "And you're in Miller? A college town? How is it that it's so hard to get drugs sold? Instead, you want to give a vampire to your drug dealer. I mean...seriously. Toby's probably happy that he's dead. Not gonna lie—you and he are like night and day. His blood was as pure and delectable as a fresh spring. You, however, I wouldn't drain your blood to water roses. You smell like a dead rat who died of lung cancer and metal poisoning. The inner lung of a ten-pack-a-day smoker. A poor excuse for a human being...a controlling, pea-brained addict who doesn't know her pockmarks from fucking holes in the ground.

"If you know what's best for you, you will stay the fuck away from me and my family, because if I catch you anywhere near my house, I will kill you on sight and get away with it."

Barbie didn't respond. She held onto her odd smile and watched Trish turn and head for her coat on the couch, proceeding with the next plan: kill bullet-less Barbie.

Trish felt her chest bloom as she healed. The ring always started on the inside and worked its way out. The ticket out of Toby's house flourished right before her eyes. Her heart slammed with heavy anticipation—that nightmare of a night was almost over. But no matter how much Trish wanted to believe the drama was close to its end and she'd be home to Darwin soon, Barbie's manic smile told Trish something else.

Trish picked up her coat and turned to pretend to head out the sliding door, when she caught an important glimpse. Barbie pulled the shotgun up, and as Trish dropped her coat and hustled to backtrack, Barbie pumped the barrel, aimed, and let off a shot.

Hot metal tore through Trish's side, ripping healing flesh free from her torso. Blood spritzed the walls, piano, island, and tile floor.

Dressed in red and pumped full of angst, Trish caught her footing and charged for Barbie, who struggled to load the weapon again. Trish threw herself into the frail girl, knocking the wind and the shotgun out of Barbie's grasp.

Both women fell to the floor, with Trish sitting on Barbie's lap. Trish sank her fingertips into the girl's face and shredded flesh, tearing Barbie's skin and muscles from her skull. Blood gushed from the new openings. The smell of raw sewage suffocated Trish, but she kept going. With every strike, the hole in her side and stomach stung less and less as her own flesh healed and reattached.

Trish's fingers tore through Barbie, ripping the fabric of something so heinous. Her nails and fingertips soaked in the woman's blood as she eviscerated her cheeks and scraped her jaw, baring bone.

The blows struck Barbie, coloring her in a crimson shock. Her eyes closed and lips pursed. Her hair mopped the spreading pool beneath them. Her arms barely fought, merely tapping Trish's knees.

But Trish bellowed a deep-throated roar, coating her bared teeth in sour blood. She grunted and her face shivered. Her nails pulled Barbie's lower eyelid down and off. Barbie's eye bulged, motionless and covered in new scars. Gashes and open wounds flooded and overflowed, hydrating exposed skull. Small islands of bruised skin remained on Barbie's forehead, but her nose and lips had gone.

Trish stopped. Breathing hard, she peered at her shaking hands. Drool streamed from her mouth, and her wet vision blurred. Bloodied skin became the muck underneath her nails, and visceral chunks wrapped her fingers.

CHAPTER 34

Escape

Feeling the effects of the serum coursing through her body, Trish welcomed accelerated healing. Her knees stiffened and her torso tingled. Her head lightened, and her belly felt less full and more satisfied. The nasty ding on her forehead and bruised lips numbed. Her nose cleared, making it easier to breathe. The wounds started closing, slowing the stream of spilling blood, reducing it to a trickle.

The ring fixed her quickly with an easy transition back to *living*. Dying was always painful, and dying while dead was literal hell. Yes, with the blood in her belly and the moon on her side, she would've healed eventually in her monstrous form. But healing would be slow, not nearly quick enough to beat the sun with her current hurt. She both loved and hated the relic. Loved it because she got to see and feel the times. Hated it because of the pure exhaustion. It was a tiredness no one could muster, compare, or feel. It was all her own.

Although the stifling, short-lived emotional and physical pain slowed her down, she pushed herself through Toby's living room and up the steps as she headed back to her original prison—the bedroom.

Trish peered around, noting the strong presence of blood and lingering sweetness from the dead preacher on the floor. Then she saw the twisted neck of a pervert lying deceased on the bed. Without having to step deep inside the scene, she turned left at the entrance and opened the top dresser drawer. Trish pulled out two V-neck t-shirts, one gray and one black. After using the black t-shirt to wipe her face and hands, she tore the bloodied dress from her body and quickly put on the gray shirt. Then she pawed around other dresser drawers until she found a pair of jogging pants. She set her clothes on the bed and marched over to the closet. As she walked, she felt her middle go numb as the serum repaired her abdominal wounds, regenerating muscle and arteries, tissue and fat. She retrieved her boots and purse from the closet and headed back to the bed.

With all her belongings in her sight, she put Darwin's picture, her credit card, and her license in her purse, along with the dirty dress and shirt. Then she put her boots on, knowing that the suede was destroyed and knowing that the night would hide the blood.

As she headed back to the hallway, a realization came down heavy on her shoulders: she wasn't done yet. More care for the scene was warranted on her part because the house and the bodies in it, the target and unannounced casualties alike, were all over the place. Any evidence of her presence was sure to lead to her capture. Miller was a small town, and everyone knew everyone. One of the church's own was dead, and so was his troubled drug-dealing cousin. A student was in the basement, crushed to death, and a pervert with his dick hanging out the front of his pants lay dead on the preacher's bed, right across from the preacher's body.

What a shit show, she thought. The media and the police would have a field day trying to solve the mystery of the woman who Toby had left the bar with. She knew they would, because the patrons at Young's would tell them so. Not only Toby's frat brothers, but the alcoholic with bad blood, the bartender, the college girl who Toby turned down for his own murderer…

Heart slamming, Trish pulled the purse from her arm and opened it. After removing the dress and the shirt, she took inventory, ensuring she had everything she'd shown up with: phone, which had a missed call from Randel, wallet, keys, the Yoga Universe membership card, the Lakeshore Public Library card, and her ring, which was still working its magic. She felt the wounds on her face close as small lingering pangs pushed through her forehead, lips, and nose.

Trish hurried to the staircase but froze halfway when high beams swung around, coating the living room curtains in a temporary brightness.

Trish went for the curtain, peering into the small gap along the left side of it. Whoever was interrupting her escape sat in the driveway next to Toby's car. Behind Toby's car was a dark minivan, which might have been Barbie's. Trish squinted at the harsh light beating brightly on the garage door. She swallowed hard as her mouth went dry and her brow moistened.

From where she stood, Trish couldn't make out who sat beneath the heavy shadows of the white sedan's cabin. But she could hear them. The stereo's subwoofers thumped against the ground. Trish presumed the driver had to be Barbie's long-awaited Steve. Little did he know that there was a massacre waiting for *him*, and when he got the nerve to head inside, Trish wanted to be long gone.

She flinched when an unfamiliar jingle erupted from somewhere behind her. Trish looked. The trifling sound came from Barbie's corpse, which lay in front of the kitchen island, missing a face. Her death probably would've hurt less and been much faster had Trish not had the ring on; she would've used claws to carve Barbie's face, not abnormally strong fingertips with normal-sized nails.

Trish backed away from the curtains and turned on her heels, opting for the other way out: the sliding door off the patio, which was just past the bloodied mess that used to be Barbie. Trish had to see who was calling; she simply couldn't resist knowing. She went for the corpse and pulled the phone from Barbie's jacket pocket.

A new text message lay over the home screen, which was a picture of Barbie from one of her better days. The woman wore a black tube dress and had her blonde hair held up in a bun. Her makeup was even decent. Barbie looked young and confident, nothing like a drugged-out hothead who manipulated people into doing things for her own benefit. No, the woman in the photo wasn't the woman who turned Trish's evening into a living hell.

Steve's text covered Barbie's midsection. It read: *Open the garage. We are here.*

Trish crushed the phone by squeezing it and tossed it in her purse. No need for anyone to see the photo Barbie had taken earlier.

Thanks for the reminder, Steve.

Trish snatched her coat up from the floor. She slid it on, keeping her purse on her shoulder and underneath the coat. She headed for the patio door, then stopped to survey the yard. She listened hard, but grimaced at the loud music from out front. Not only did it make it hard to hear, but it also grabbed attention; she could tell. The sleepy neighborhood seemed to be in the middle-upper-class bracket. Those people worked early mornings. They'd call the police soon if they hadn't already because of the gunshots and shouting. And now, the loud music. She felt it in her flipping gut. Time was almost out.

Trish stepped out onto the patio, leaving the door open behind her. She hustled down the steps and ran across the grass in a back yard that seemed to go on forever. Trish cringed at the noisy crushing sounds erupting underneath her feet as she trekked through dead leaves. Chest tightening, she watched the tree line approach slowly. Almost relieved, she sucked in a gulp of fresh air, and her body quaked with every knock from her rushing heart.

She burst through the tree line, finding herself surrounded by bare, limping branches and colorful leaves.

More leaves. More noise. With the deceased forestry encasing the ground, anyone could track and spot her. She secretly hoped Steve hadn't left his car, and she was sure he hadn't. Trish didn't hear a door slam, and the music stayed at the same volume, decreasing with distance.

Don't stop. Don't look back. Just keep going. You're free.

She had almost lost feeling in her legs, but she rejoiced. The overhead lights in the construction site lit up the night in the short distance, just on the other side of the trees. It cast a halo over the campus, prominent in the twilight as it got closer. Trish ran on hot heels while gasping for breath.

The finish line drew near.

The finish line was there.

Almost. Al—

"Stop!" someone said.

Her heart sank, but her legs kept moving.

A flying bullet nicked a nearby tree coming up in her path, forcing her to slide to a stop, which took her balance. Her legs went up and her feet went flying as she landed on her back.

CHAPTER 35

Questions

Trish clawed at the ground, struggling to stand. The frosted leaves slipped from her palms as she tried catching a grip of the soft, uneven earth. She managed to get on her knees, but before she could stand, a darkened silhouette was upon her, aiming another damned gun in her face.

"Get on your feet," he said, his tenor close to a whisper. "*Slowly*."

She planted one foot and pushed herself up. Trish glared at the starry sky, watching her frosty breath escape into the atmosphere.

"Put your hands up," he said.

Trish lifted her hands. She rolled her eyes and accepted her new reality: the night wasn't over. And as she felt her blood leak less, her aches simmering down to minor pains, she cursed her decision to have ever stepped foot back into Miller.

As he approached, the frosty clouds from his breathing blinded her to what she thought to be a desolate forest.

But it wasn't desolate.

The man walked circles around her, keeping his pistol aimed at her with one hand, stroking his pale, bare chin with the other. His short bangs hung over his forehead, and his black hood covered the sides of his thin face. He searched with intrigue and studied with intent, his gray eyes glistening with wonder. His skin smelled like woody cologne and a freshly lit joint.

"I'm happy I caught you," he said. "Otherwise, I would've had to hunt you down." His boots crushed foliage, and the foul scent of stale blood became more apparent as he drew closer. This man was a killer, and his name had to be Steve.

"I gotta admit, you're pretty fast," he said, his words easy and steady. "I mean, you're not as fast as I thought a vampire would be… Maybe just as fast as a track star, but you are fast."

He patted her hips down and rubbed her belly. She cringed, her body aching at his touch, still raw and embracing the healing process.

"I just wanna make sure you're not hiding anything, Ms. Vampire. I don't plan on dying today—well *ever*, actually."

Ever? Trish froze. Chills ran down her back. The cold metal neared her skin from behind, and she tensed when the gun clicked, loading the chamber. He pushed it deep into the nape of her neck.

"Just know that if you move, I will shoot. Is that clear?" he asked.

Trish ground the backs of her teeth. There was nothing worse than a person like him with a gun. Based on what Danny had said, Steve was unstable. He might've tried to murder her until he actually did. Then, he'd probably drink her blood to *never die*, as he'd put it. Although Trish was healing, she couldn't take another blow. So, she stood still and listened to the man.

Luckily, she *was* healing.

"A mutual friend told me all about you, and I had to come see for myself. You know that they thought I knew you?"

Silence.

"Do you talk?" he asked.

Trish didn't say anything. She only thought about her coming escape and how she'd have to leave another body behind. Trish would have to; she was already out of time. The question was when and how she could pull it off in the next few minutes. She moved her eyes, hoping not to find anyone else lurking about. He seemed to be alone.

"So, is that a no?" he asked.

He's not going to let up. It'd be best to— "What's it matter?" she quipped, tired of the conversation and exhausted with the evening.

"She speaks! *Hallelujah!*"

"How long have you been back here?" she asked, wondering what he'd seen.

He chuckled.

"How did you get back here? Who's in the car?" she asked.

"Oh, that there is just one of my friends. He offered me a ride, but I decided to walk. It's a nice night out, and I don't live too far away. Nobody lives too far away in Miller—seven minutes to the farthest edges of town, ya know?" He smacked his lips. "Well, that, and I had to make sure Barbie wasn't lying about finding a vampire. I had to surprise her with my exact arrival. I heard she's been lying a lot lately, so logistics and all…"

"Look, I don't know what she told you, but she's lying. I'm not a vampire. I'm just an escort looking for my way out of this shithole," Trish said, minding the fact Steve could've been as high as Barbie. He certainly smelled like it. Playing with his state of mind could be her way out.

"Oh really?" He moved around a little, jostling the barrel of the gun and reaching in his hoodie for something. Steve walked around front, holding the gun to her face now. He lifted his phone up with his free hand, the screen facing her. There was a picture of her in Toby's bed, chained down at the wrists and ankles, anger ingrained in her face as Barbie used her raunchy fingers to lift Trish's upper lip. Her fangs sat on display for the psycho before her to see. "Those fangs in your mouth say otherwise, and I think you should know that I hate liars. I hate them so much that I tear them open to figure out how they tick. What makes them *lie*? Now, not only are you a liar, but you are also a monster…an immortal monster—you can give me things. Many, many things." He smiled. "Think of *all the possibilities*. But the first thing I want from you, though, is the truth. And I mean the truth about everything that I ask you. All right?"

Trish sighed.

He shook his head slowly. "See, it doesn't feel like we understand each other. So, I'll reiterate. If you don't answer my questions, I'll just shoot you right here and go in there to find answers myself. I don't want to have to do that. I don't want to take on that risk, but I will do just that."

Feeling the small shake in his voice was evidence enough. He *would* pull the trigger and, at the very least, leave her with a head wound in the woods. She shook her head, then said, "I wouldn't go back in there if I were you. The poli—"

"I don't give a fuck about the cops. I own them, just like I own everything in this town. I own the college, I own the people, I own the church…and right now, I own you. Now, are you going to answer my questions, or do I have to find the answers myself?"

Trish tensed, unnerved by her options. He might not have been as idiotic as Barbie. In fact, he seemed much more dangerous than what she was told. "Can you just…put the gun down?"

He laughed. "Really? Why would I do that?"

Trish cocked her head. She'd rather he dropped the gun to make things easier. Make it easy to put him out of his misery by making it look like a drug deal gone wrong. The murders would be on his shoulders, not hers, and the last threat would be removed.

"Nah. I can't put the gun down. But you can answer my question. Or I'll put a bullet in your head. I mean, you might not die, but it would be worth it to find out for sure, don't you think?"

She cringed. The comparisons to media vampires turned her stomach upside down at the mere mention of them. But in this case, he wasn't wrong…maybe.

"Are you immortal?" he asked.

"I don't know, but I never died before, sooo…"

"That's funny, because I've also never died before," he said through a barrage of laughter. He cleared his throat. "Are they dead in there?"

"What?" she quipped, not sure what to say.

"Are they all dead in there?" he asked slower.

"I—"

"Before you lie, just remember what I said about liars."

She pursed her lips and strained at the throat. "Yes."

"Did you kill them?"

Trish didn't speak. She only watched the barrel, waiting for it to blow. But she didn't have a reason to lie. Or to tell the truth. "No. I hid most of the time."

"I find that hard to believe."

"What do you mean?"

"Well, when I look at you, I see someone in trouble. Someone with something to hide. Aside from your clothes looking a lot different from that bloody dress you had on in the picture, you're running away from that house"—he pointed in the direction of Toby's house with his free hand—"at full speed, and Barbie isn't answering her phone. She always answers the phone when she's expecting me. So even when you rushed across the yard and disappeared into the tree line, I *watched* you. I know you killed them because you crept out the back door like...well, a *creep*. Right?"

Trish could only think about how she was going to kill *him*. Leaving his body there, just past the tree line outside the house, was perfect.

"So, I see you don't want to say," Steve said. "You know what? I can respect that. You see, even though you are a lying sack of shit, you get to be because you're different. Unique. And I mean it, *truly unique*. Like a piece of rare art. I mean...when they sent me the picture of you, I stared...and...I was baffled, *truly* taken by something beautiful. I stared at the picture for a long time. Could've been an hour. I...I don't know. I just couldn't take my eyes off the most gorgeous species to bless this earth. You're amazing, and you should know that. I mean, you probably already know that. It feels good to talk to you, really. And moreover, you can't die. You're fucking immortal. You...you are history. You've probably seen so much—done so much. Been to so many places."

He watched her, still pointing the barrel in her face.

"You know, we aren't too different, me and you. People fear us because they don't understand us. You feed on their blood to live. You suck on their life's essence to fill your own. You are...real magic. *Extraterrestrial.*"

With all the strange talk and claims of magnificence, internally, Trish begged Steve to pull the trigger. He sounded a lot like her ex, Victor, who'd paid her to suck his blood as some sort of sick kink. She'd do it for a short time only. Enough time for minute amounts of venom to ride his blood stream, not enough to turn him, and not enough to kill him...

"I mean, they call me the mad scientist, the drug dealer, the bringer of death and disaster, but they don't know that there is more to me. More than they would *ever* know. I'm intelligent. I'm mystical, innovative. Probably one of the biggest thinkers of our time." He looked her over again, intrigue blooming in his eyes, and he lowered the barrel. "But you're more than that, and seeing you is like finding a unicorn. Thank you for blessing me with your presence. Thank you."

"Are you going to let me go?" Trish asked.

"Yeah." He nodded. "Yeah. For sure—for now." A half-manic smile crossed his deviant mug. "But I will find you. And when I do, I will trap you. And then, eventually, I will *kill* you."

"Is that a threat?" she asked, taming her pride. She couldn't afford another bullet to the body.

"Look, Barbie was a piece of work—a piece of shit, really. I can't argue with that. And oh, did she love to stick those dirty fingers in the pot. I mean, what can I say? The woman loved her drugs. But I had a soft spot for her. You know those fuck-ups that you wish you could see do better? But you know that they *won't* do better? That was what she was to me. I cared for her more than her own family. I *loved* her. She was like a little cousin to me. I would say sister, but—" He chuckled. "I would hate to be that close to her in the bloodline. I don't know what I'd do if I inherited those teeth. But anyway, she was my dear friend. Killing her is the same as stealing money from my pocket. I mean, she brought in friends from all over the place. She might've looked like shit, but the girl spent almost every weekend in almost every trailer park across the state. She was the Trailer Park Queen. She..."

His face hardened, and he fell into deep thought.

"And then Tay," he went on. "He...he was like a little brother, man. He... How you... To Tay. He was *young*. He was in school. I don't give a fuck about Danny, but Tay?"

"So why not just kill me now?" Trish asked.

"The other vampire asked me the same thing."

Trish's face crumbled. "Another—"

"As a kid, I'd take my fake foam sword and slay fake dragons and the Boogie Man. I'd kill thieves and play double agent to the FBI. I was always victorious in taking down some of the more notorious. I kind of do that now. Why don't you think we have homeless people in Miller? Well, homeless drug addicts? I am a hero, and I do get rewarded for it. But this…this is a dream come true. No way I'd go to prison for killing monsters. Hell, people would give me a fucking medal for it. *Steve, The Vampire Killer*. It has a nice ring to it, huh? You can't say, in your long existence, that you haven't caused any pain or killed the young. So not only will I put a mythical monster down, but I'll also use your body to help me figure out immortality. So many possibilities."

"So, back to my original question," Trish said, reminding him of her only concern, not his weird dreams.

"I feel like it would be more fun to hunt you down. This is too easy for me. I need a real challenge, you get me?"

Trish couldn't tell if he was high or not. His blood didn't smell as bad as Barbie's, and the scent of his skin was more like death soaked in perfume than drug abuse. But it didn't matter. Trish wanted the conversation to end, and the idea of turning around and redoing that night was far off base. She had to get home.

She winced at the idea of leaving another loose end out in the open, but there was an up-side—Steve wouldn't tell anyone, leaving him as the only loose end. Him and his *vampiric* friend. Still, she had to be sure.

"How do I know that you won't go to the police?" she asked.

"Because they take the fun out of everything."

"But you own the police, right? How do I know you won't—"

"Hey, hey, *hey*. The police I'm talking about ain't cops. They're dirty pigs looking for a payday. That's all. Don't worry, I wouldn't hand you over to them…alive, anyway. I don't snitch—not even on my enemies."

He holstered his gun and opened his hands, showing her they were empty and he was no longer a threat.

"Go ahead. I'm sure you need to be indoors before the sun comes up. I wouldn't want my dream destroyed because she melted away."

Steve winked at her and took off running in the opposite direction.

PART 7

Homebound

CHAPTER 36

A New Crisis

Trish darted through the thick woodland encompassing Miller University just after crossing the dark street, leaving the residential area behind her. She felt a little better as the serum pumped viable blood through her organs. She had watched herself heal before and documented her assumptions. Her blood was different from what made a human...human. An unknown compound flowed through her arteries and veins, healing and strengthening her skin against the stubborn sun. But healing happened faster when she sat still, allowing whatever energy her body reproduced to distribute easily.

While fleeing and afraid, she felt subtle spasms tug at her side and gut, right in the wound Barbie had torn into her. Trish slowed to a brisk limp, hoping for her body to mend a little faster. Hoping the crippling gouge regenerated enough for her to get out of Miller before the police got wise to what happened at Toby's house.

Her mind reeled on the words of a psycho: *Another vampire.*
Victoria Scott?

Steve crept through Trish's thoughts, along with his threat and promise.

He's going to hunt me, she thought, quickening her steps and crossing the construction zone.

Her nose flared. *Bring it, bitch.* She'd been hunted before— Steve was no different from anyone else. She only hoped he didn't find her home. Hoped that he didn't find Darwin. She frowned and her face flushed. *Shit. Steve could find Darwin.*

Trish groaned and slowed down again, crushing progress with slow steps. She felt bits of bullet push through her ripped skin as it closed, reserving blood. Twisted nerves fought her aggressive movements, exacerbating the pain.

But she didn't stop, even though she wished she had. There was no time to pick up the bits of bullet sliding from her abdomen.

No. Someone might see me. Hiding her identity was more important than digging through the grass for bullet fragments. *And there's no DNA*, she reminded herself. *It'll just be spent bullets from a gun at the crime scene. Nothing more.*

The night sounds of the rural college campus had a way of playing with the imagination. She wasn't sure if it was the slamming of her anxious heart or blood loss, but her heels went hot in her haste, as if someone were chasing after her. Trish looked over her shoulder, finding the construction site growing smaller behind her. The heat on the back of her neck made her try harder to hurry.

Orange and yellow leaves illuminated in the night. The breeze whipped around, feeling good as her body adjusted, giving her nerve endings the ability to feel the cold again. Healing had taken her, soothing over the bits of flesh stolen by bullets and chases, accidents and naivety.

Trish felt herself pick up speed, running toward the full moon's round glow.

Almost there.

With newfound exuberance, she thought about Darwin and how much she needed to see him. She thought about Randel and wished he were home. Trish wanted to hold her family while they slept, unaware and innocent.

Hopefully Darwin doesn't go through this. Maybe he was only experimenting with his teeth. He didn't mean to bite that kid... He didn't mean to bite me this morning, either. He's human. A human who she just put in danger. There was no telling what other pictures Barbie sent over to Steve; she could have easily sent Darwin's.

Trish ran across parking lots and along the backend of quiet dorms before catching sight of Young's parking lot. It was empty, and the streets had cleared, with the occasional shouting in the distance. Lights lined the walkways, glowing in the night. She avoided them the best she could by running faster, although there was no one around to see.

Another vampire. Steve's voice rang out once more. His words messed with her head, making her look over her shoulder again. There was nothing.

She didn't understand why Steve didn't make his move right then and there. Was he really trying to play a game? *Is Victoria the other vampire?*

The new questions took hold in Trish's mind, angering her as she crossed the vacant street and headed to the Jeep, careful not to catch the camera, if it worked at all.

CHAPTER 37

Wheelbarrow Wheels

The storage unit felt desolate at such a late hour, 2:31 a.m. to be exact. Bright silver lights lit up the parking lot and the entrance to the tower of storage units. There were no cars, and Earl had gone for the night, leaving the supplementary single-story building empty. Trish made her way inside, back to her personal space.

She scrubbed the blood off her face, wincing as her skin was still raw to the touch. She pulled off her clothes and assessed the damage. Her nose had reddened, no longer busted or crushed. Her lips were chapped as they shed bruised skin. The bruises on her forehead, cheek, and shoulder had shrunk to dim blemishes. The stab wound on her left side looked more like a pink streak, or a scratch, and the shotgun wound was reduced to moles that were speckled along her left side.

Any semblance of injury and hurt from that night would disappear by the morning, thanks to her ring. She took solace in that familiar notion. Ally had given her one of the greatest gifts that she'd ever received, and she'd killed for it.

***

Things hadn't gotten any easier for Trish by May 1890. As she dragged herself through the woods, she questioned if it had always been so hard to find food. The winter had been unforgiving. She

196

didn't suffer from frostbite, but exposure to the elements on an empty stomach made her feel weak. After she'd eaten the wolf months earlier, the sunburns and bites had subsided after a week of lying in a wet, dank cave. But soon after, her body crumbled in pain, forcing her to find more food.

Trish couldn't remember how many nights she walked, and how many days she spent in an occasional hollowed-out tree stump or mountain wall cave. What she did during the day didn't feel like sleep. When she closed her eyes, she was back in the woods with trees that were not green, and a sky that wasn't blue. Black leaves and branches hung from the weeping willows that bled red sap from the crevices ingrained in the thick trunk. Black clouds floated about in the red sky. A small, faraway sun barely lit up the forest floor, which felt like pounds of soft ash underneath Trish's feet. The air smelled of burning iron and flesh, and she couldn't help but to force her mouth open, taking it all in like a fish in oxygen-rich water. Even as she walked around in her daydreams, she could still hear the very real woods that surrounded her hiding place. Birds sang and flies lingered. Nature was alive, and it taunted her with its daytime calls.

Her body knew when night had arrived because her red forest changed. Red snowflakes fell onto her tongue, and they tasted like blood. She rejoiced and shouted at the heavens to send more, promised that she'd dance for it. And she did. The clouds would break open and send down a deluge of red snow, none of which was cold on her skin, all of which filled her belly.

But when Trish woke up to her reality, deep in her hiding spot, she crawled out and continued into the darkness of a forest that wasn't red, but black in the night. Her limbs turned into bones as all her fat disappeared; she saw her joints where her bones met.

She walked past the mountainside and noticed that the air was thicker in her throat and that the land had gone flat; West Virginia had fallen behind her. She wasn't at home anymore. Panicked, she shed a tear as she ventured deeper into the unknown, closing in on a piece of the country that was foreign to her. The leaves were a different type of green, lighter and perkier. The grass was softer, shorter. The flowers looked more like dandelions and weeds. She stopped, contemplating going back to a place she knew. Back to a hiding spot, because she wasn't sure of the time, but morning would be flooding the horizon soon enough. But her eyes found something else. There was a deer feeding alone in a flat clearing. Its antlers were long and plentiful. Its body was thick and tall, and she imagined that it was a full-grown male. She looked around and found no herd lingering about. No small prey that would be easier to take down in her own decrepit state.

With nothing else in sight, she trained her eyes on the mammal. After what felt like months of searching for rabbits, chipmunks, and wolves, she wasn't allowing the deer to leave unscathed. Her fangs elongated, filling her mouth with venom as she skulked on tiptoes, creeping up on the unsuspecting feasting animal.

She approached it from behind, fully intending to jump on its back and plunge her fangs into its neck. *Finally, finally,* she thought, a giddy smirk spreading across her lips. The hunger and cravings would be—

The deer lifted its muscular hind legs and shoved its hooves into her chest, stealing her breath and sending her flying a few feet until her back slammed into a nearby tree. The crack in her ears deafened her to the night songs around her as she fell forward on her belly.

The deer trampled the ground as it ran off, leaving her behind. She went to turn on her back, but her body screamed as agonizing pangs rode the length of her extremities. She couldn't move her shoulders or hips; there was no feeling. Her back was numb, and her neck was stiff. The stars watched her back as she cried. Debilitating aches slowly crept into her back and chest and her stomach buckled.

As she lay there, face in the grass, Trish missed home. But there was no going back, not as she was. Momma wouldn't understand. The townsmen, who were quick to grab pitchforks and guns, wouldn't understand. And she was sure that they were out looking for her, or at least they had been out all winter hoping to recover her body. With all the blood and carnage left behind in the coop, the town may have declared her *eaten alive.*

Pained and malnourished, Trish felt as drained as a person ever could. She coughed and spat up blood, then groaned as her rattled lungs sent aches through her tortured torso. But as the darkness took on a blue hue, and the stars disappeared, she willed herself to move.

"No, no, no!" she cried. "Come on," she grunted. The sky faded to burnt orange, and panic squeezed her chest. She shook, willing herself to stand up, willing herself to move to the nearest shade. "Come on," she cried.

The first sun rays burned her fingertips, and she shrieked. And yet, she could not move, could not push off the abusive light even though every nerve ending in her hand begged for protection.

"No, no! Help me please!" The skin on her fingers began to boil and split as the rays found her forearms and penetrated her boots. She shrieked, deafening herself to the surrounding woods.

"No, no, nope." A deep raspy voice from somewhere she couldn't see. He brought about a strong scent of sweet tobacco and sweat. Then his footsteps rescinded, pounding the soft grass.

Her breath caught in her chest as her back roasted in new sun rays. "Help," she cried.

The stranger returned with something that squeaked.

She saw the black cover before she saw the man who had been holding it as he covered her. It was scratchy and thick, and it covered her head and neck and back. It shielded her legs and ankles and feet.

"This'll help," he mumbled. "Better, I bet it feels *way* better. Better than-than a hot bath. Better-better than an open flame in a bonfire." He rolled her over, wrapping her in the cover. Then she felt him put strong arms underneath her and lift. He tucked her body into what felt like a large metal bowl.

Wheelbarrow? As he pulled her along, the wheels beneath her creaked and kicked up dusty earth. They crushed sweet grass and splashed standing water puddles.

"Nah, these don't belong out here in the morning or afternoon. Turn-turn into beef jerky or skin soup," he said.

She wasn't sure who he was speaking to, and only briefly did she wonder what his intentions were. But as they continued, she found herself back in her bloody forest, where she walked around with an open mouth to the red sky, and the sound of old, creaking wheelbarrow wheels in her ears.

CHAPTER 38

Bath

Trish woke with a start, her chest tightening and head throbbing as she sat up. Her face crumbled at the abhorrent smell of rotten eggs. Then her arms flailed, and her hands smacked the water that surrounded her, soaking her bare skin. Water splashed and spilled from the metal tub and onto the wooden floor. She stopped, but her heart quaked, beating louder than drums, louder than thunder in her ears. She looked down at her unsummoned bath and her eyes widened. There were no bubbles, only water that stopped beneath her breasts. She wondered how long she'd been there, because she didn't feel the temperature on her skin; couldn't tell if it was hot or cold.

"Where am I?" she whispered. She thought back. She saw fur, felt hunger, then hooves impaled her chest. She looked down at her chest. Her pale skin looked smooth, absent of red splits and purple bruises.

She looked at the shaken surface of the water and remembered landing on her belly. Then there was the sun.

Trish lifted her shoulders and then relaxed them, noting no pain in her back. Realizing that she could move. Her eyes widened as she looked at her hands and lifted her legs from the water. Her limbs bared no burns. Even the blemishes that riddled her knees and arms were gone. She felt her face, and it was smooth and clean, no grime or cuts. She dropped her hands back into the water and gawked at the dark wooden wall just past the metal tub. She was like new again, the way she'd been before she left home, before life turned into death and confusion. Hunger and distress.

Her throat tightened as she took in her surroundings. There was a wooden table against the wall behind her, and in front of her there were two tables against the wall that was adjacent to the tub. Glass bottles and weird-shaped cups and flasks with red, clear, or yellow liquid took up the surface. Smoke bellowed from steel canisters that had a small door on the base and an opening on top. Trish attributed the horrific smell to whatever had been cooking in what sounded like boiling water. There were also strange metal instruments that held fat-bottomed flasks over naked flames. Glass cups with powders and shiny silver, gold, and copper shavings lined the shelves stationed over each table, and an assortment of cast-iron spoons and spatulas hung on each wall.

On the wall opposite the tub was a bookshelf full of books with a small table and a single chair in front of it. She didn't care to try to read the titles on the spines; she didn't speak the language. She cocked her head, remembering the man who helped her. He mumbled to himself in English.

"You weren't careful; you're sloppy, messy. Got real careless," the familiar voice said.

Trish flinched, finding the man standing at the door. His leathery, tanned face was blank, unassuming, and uncurious. His salt and copper hair was pulled back, and he wore a white cotton top and beige slacks. Even though he seemed like a normal person who may have spent too much time in the sun, he had a golden aura about him, shining as he stood in the dim doorway.

She watched him move about; the smell of sweet tobacco followed him along. He marched over to the counter and stuck his finger into the water bath. Then he pulled a glass tube from the roiling waters.

"Should almost be about done, don't ya think?"

Trish folded her arms over her chest and crossed her legs, her heart racing at the thought of all he'd seen. She imagined herself blushing, but, just as she had noticed months before, she was incapable of feeling anything other than pain and confusion. No hot flushed cheeks or nippy cold nights—only the burning sun that tore into her with its small fiery blades.

"Ah. You're ready-ready to dry off. Ready to get out of the bath." He replaced the test tube and headed out of the room. He returned with a thick cloth and faced the bookshelf while extending his arm out to her, offering her the towel.

She quickly stood and took the towel, and he chuckled. "Like I haven't seen it before. Like I don't know what a *woman* looks like. You know how many women I've seen? There was Haidi May down in Port City. I helped her deliver her blood child."

Blood child? Trish thought, as she wrapped the towel around her body. Only then did her body ache with hunger pains.

"Then there was Patty Toll, who needed a silver bullet removed from her liver and thigh. Then Joyce Maynard, a runaway slave who had a run-in with the church."

Trish decided to let her hair drip dry. She didn't need to be naked any longer than she already had been in front of the man.

"That-that was hard to see, but I fixed her up real good…sent her on her way to Akron and she…yeah. She sent signals 'specially for me, but I told her that there was no way I was leaving these here foothills. Told her Pennsylvania is my *home*. Always. Always. Always."

Hm, Trish thought, surprised that she'd walked that far.

He turned and smiled at her. "And now I'm going to help you."

She swallowed and tilted her head. "How—" She coughed, her dry throat itchy. She realized that she hadn't used her voice other than to sob and scream over the last several months.

His eyebrows drew together. Then he put up a finger and left the room. He returned and held out some clothes for her. "I fixed your dress—made it like new. But I hate to say that it won't protect you from the all-seeing star. I mean, you should know that by now, cause when I found you, the sun had been seeing you pretty good over the last couple weeks—" He looked at her again. "Or months."

She took the dress and surveyed it. The blood was gone, and he'd patched up the holes with a cloth that was either a few shades too light or too dark, a far cry from the original burgundy color.

"Thank you," she said bashfully as she pulled the dress on. She wasn't sure whether to run or learn more about the stranger. He'd helped her in ways that she thought impossible from a normal person. *Is he normal?* She found herself looking him up and down. His clothes were normal. His skin was more golden than she'd ever seen, but maybe that was a Pennsylvania thing? She wasn't sure.

"You're so very welcome. My name is Ally. And you are?"

"Patricia."

"Nice to meet you. I know a Patricia. Nice lady, kind lady. Can I call you Trish?"

She shrugged, feeling that the name had a ring to it and not wanting to curse the name that Momma had given her. It didn't feel right to describe the thing that she had become with her original name; the label was no longer fitting.

His face somehow brightened as his perfect smile spread even wider. "Hey, do you notice anything different?"

She narrowed her eyes. "What?" Her pulse quickened. There it was. He saved her because he had done something *to* her. She felt her fingertips tingle and her gums numb.

"When I found you, you were covered in cuts and bruises. And that deer who hangs out in that clearing over there kicked the hell out of ya."

"You see it kick me?" she asked, her voice hoarse.

"No, but Heath is notorious for kicking the shit out of anybody that comes close to his part of the forest. He—" Ally rubbed the back of his neck. "He lost a lot of family and friends over the years. A bit insecure, if you ask me—convinced that everyone is out to get him."

"The deer?" She shook her head, getting back on the subject. "What's different about me? What'd you do to me?" Her questions came out ruder than she intended, but she needed to know before she left the strange man behind for good.

"Oh, yes! Uh…how do you think those bruises and broken bones disappeared?"

She looked at the undisturbed bath water.

He quickly shook his head. "Nope. That tub was only used for cleaning you up and giving you somewhere to sleep."

"Okay…?" She felt her claws erect, ready to tear skin from Ally's pathetic smiling face. Only then did her gut erupt in cramps that made her bend at the waist.

"Oh! I almost forgot." He headed for the wooden table that was adjacent to the tub. He pulled a flask from one of the canisters, smoking water dripping from the bottom of the glass. "How negligent of me. Thinking that anyone can function—focus—consider on an empty stomach. Here." The cork made a popping sound when he removed it. The smell of iron and flesh cloaked the room, killing the sulfuric and tobacco scent. Her fangs buried themselves into her lower lip as the sweet venom drowned her tonsils. Her claws had stopped sliding from her nail beds, fully grown and ready to slice. He quickly handed her the flask.

"Wha's this?" she asked, her mouth ready to drip on her chin.

"If you drink, it will help you. I promise." It was difficult to read the sincerity in his dark eyes, but it was there. All seriousness, and his clear tone said as much. Ally was unfazed by her fangs and claws. He hadn't gone for a torch or a gun. He had offered her something that her body yearned for, and she couldn't explain the new urge, not even if she tried. She took the flask and drank. It was thicker and cleaner than that of the wolf's. It was fuller and meatier, sweet, bitter, and salty all at once. It had a well-rounded taste, and her body thanked her for it. She slowed down only to catch her breath.

"There was a man by the name of Morgan Gunther," Ally said as he eased back to the table in front of the bookcase and sat on the edge. "He ran a farm just over seventy miles east of here. Morgan wasn't a good man—was a con—a liar—and Morgan had a habit of betting his ass until he lost it."

She let the silence linger between them as she went on drinking.

"Just be happy that you didn't have to do the hard part. Harvesting can be really tricky—dangerous…sometimes impossible."

She gulped and stopped drinking. She dropped her shoulders and scowled at the jug as if it were poison.

"Harvesting is essential to your survival. That's what those there fangs are for—to bite." He tapped the side of his neck. "Always aim for the jugulars. There are three pairs—six in all—to choose from.

There's that, and don't get caught." He raised a finger. "And don't waste time on kids. They're too small, and the people—they'll come after you real quick. Before-before you can sink your fangs in. Luckily, you can drink right now because you don't have to harvest—I did that for you. But that will never be the case again."

"This…this belong to someone?" she yelled.

He nodded slowly. "Now you're getting it."

Trish dropped the flask, sending blood and glass scattering across the floor. She rushed over to the tub and shoved water into her mouth.

CHAPTER 39

Gold

"Stop," Ally said as he continued leaning against the table. He watched Trish with intent, almost like Momma had when Trish was over-exaggerating her tiredness or a scraped knee.

"No," she declared between exasperated wet breaths as she continued washing her mouth out.

"Look, it's too late—there's no going back—reversing the tide. You are what you are. Now stop acting like a child—a babe—and tell me how you feel."

"Disgusting," she shouted before she gurgled the water, trying and failing to knock the taste out of her mouth. She spit it out and asked, "This how you healed me?"

"No. No, I didn't, because if I did, then you would have surely choked on it. I can assure you that much. No. I used something else entirely. Rubbed a little on your wounds, and just like magic, the formula healed you up good."

She stopped rinsing her mouth in the tub and turned to face him. "I-I don't understand."

He pointed at the canister that was holding a glass tube. "You've been meditating for three days," he said. "While you were out, the serum healed your skin and bones, but it didn't feed you-fill you with sustenance. No. But ol' Morgan did."

"No," she said as she wept. How did she drink human blood and enjoy it? "No, dis...dis ain't me!" she shrilled. She slid down the side of the tub and sat on the floor. Then she pulled her legs into the fetal position. She rocked. "No." Her body quavered as her heart raced. She enjoyed the blood. She wanted more. And it was all she would ever want. The taste and texture clung to her mind. The smell and sight of it on the floor made her want to lick it clean. But she cried instead.

Ally kneeled before her. "Tell me, little monster, when you close your eyes to kill time, what do you see?"

"I-I—"

"What do you see, feel, smell, hear, taste? Is it blood? When you're trapped in your deepest thoughts, do you feed on what you desire? What you want?"

She glared at him. "Yes," her voice cracked. "I'm jus' like the thing that killed me. And now, dat's all I wanna do. I wanna kill someone and drain 'em. Not only cause I'm hungry, but cause I wan' them to suffer like I did. But I'd show mercy." She nodded frantically. "I'd make sure dey don't get back up." She wailed and shook her head. *I'mma killer*, she thought. *I'mma monster.* "Why? Why you help me? You know what I am?"

"Oh," he whispered in a conspiring hush. "Of course I know who you are. I know what you have become. You-you are a blood sucker. A vampire."

She shook her head, as if shaking the observation loose from her memory. "Those ain't real," she spat.

"Well, I'm looking and even talking to one right now, ain't I?" He said *ain't* using a country accent, almost sounding like Josef. "Pretty girl like you shoulda stayed indoors instead of fussin' aroun' inna dark. Damn monsta din gotcha pretty li'l neck."

She pictured Momma saying the same thing over and over. Trish only wished she got to go back home to take the tongue lashing. But she knew that would never happen. "Stop it."

"Oh, don't cry. It's not my job to persecute you. If you are unlucky-unfortunate, those people out there will do enough of that."

She considered him again and found comfort in his easy eyes. Ally wasn't scared of the truth, welcoming her to join in on it. She couldn't imagine anyone being as accepting as he…unless he wanted something in return. She furrowed her brow. "Who are you?"

"A recluse," he said. "A recluse who knows a lot of chemical and metal tricks." He smiled. "I know a lot about a lot. Especially rare things and beings."

She blinked away tears. "Like what?"

"Oh, a lot of things," he said. "For instance, I know Santa and the Easter Bunny aren't real. Sorry, but most of those characters that bring children joy are not real. You're old enough to know that though. Like the tooth fairy or the leprechaun that shits out gold—he doesn't shit out gold. He collects body parts and sells them for gold." He rolled his eyes as if everyone should have shared that knowledge. "But don't worry, they rip and run around Europe. Not here in the US. They think Americans are barbaric."

Trish raised a brow; she was sure that Ally was messing with her.

"But you, my dear, are a rarity, and how do people treat rarities? Like precious relics, right? Something that should be maintained for as long as the earth itself. Right?"

"I'm nobody's prop," she said.

"No. A prop must have a user. You are your own user."

"I—"

"It's been a while since I've seen one of you." He frowned as if an epiphany had hit him square in the face. "Tell me what happened."

"The town was talkin' 'bout somethin'…some monster that killed livestock and…and I guess they found it. They chased it 'round and tortured it 'cause it was burnt and beat up when it bit me. It killed me."

"Where is it? What happened to it?" Trish sensed worry weighing on his tone.

She shook her head. "Dead. They hanged it. It-it's gon'. Just like me. I'm gon'. I-I'll never see my momma again. I—"

His face relaxed, falling into a familiar smile. "Shh. Shh. It's alright. You're not dead. You are awakened. You are alive, more alive than any normal human. And just like people and animals and stars, you deserve to live. Just as intended."

"Nobody wanna monster around. Nobody—"

"No one is God. *We* are God. We decide who exists. The earth decides who lives on it. Not a magician, but a rock. And you…you are here. You defy the odds. You beat the sun for months. You won because you made it here. And now, you get a prize."

He went back to the canister and replaced the test tube. Then he grabbed the cast-iron tongs from the wall. He looked over his shoulder at her. "I think gold would look good on you." He pulled a gold bracelet from the water bath and set it on the table. He poked it, then picked it up.

"Let me see your arm."

She did.

He clamped the bracelet around her wrist. The flickering flames of the lanterns shone in the golden finish.

"Breathe," he said.

She did.

"Try to only take it off once a season. A full-grown adult should be enough to get you through three months. Since you are so small, that is more than enough time to digest. Follow that schedule, and you'll have plenty of serum to get you through the next two centuries."

She wasn't confident about that, confident that she shouldn't live that long. Was she allowed?

"Ah, you'll be fine," he said, as if reading her mind. "Here is a hint: you are a pretty woman, and you turned at such a young age. That's enough to get any unsuspecting man alone. And I am sure you know that you are strong. You can take any human down with your new bone density. Use that. Use all of that."

She studied the bracelet. It was the finest piece of anything that she'd ever had. Her limbs felt lighter, and her nerves relaxed. Trish floated on air, back in a body that she had known for the longest. A body before death. "But—what is it?"

"I call it *Life's Essence*. It turns you into them, those who prosecute you. Those who tell you that you don't belong amongst them on a planet that belongs to all of us."

She looked at him, unsure.

"Come here," he said as he headed for the door. "I want to show you something."

They stepped out into the main room. This room had a window, while the lab did not, and it looked a lot like her cabin back in West Virginia. But the space was much smaller. There was a single bed, a fireplace, and a wood stove. He even had another table with two oak chairs against it, a red and black plaid loveseat, and another lantern on the floor. Trish remained in the doorway, her face twisted at the idea of stepping into the room; it was drenched in yellow light

"Don't be afraid, come on."

She shook her head in protest. Trish was sure that the sun-bleached room would kill her.

He put a hand on his hip. "If I was going to kill you, I would've done it three days ago. If I was going to burn you in the sun, I would have left you out there to die. But I didn't. Now please, come into the light. I promise it will not hurt you."

As she reached a toe into the room, the stinging and burning sensation that had plagued her for months was absent.

"See?" he exclaimed.

She stepped into the room completely, taking in the warmth without pain and scorn.

"It's all thanks to that." He pointed to the bracelet. "The serum is inside, pushing life into your pores and into your blood. Controlling your hormones and immunity. It's…my best discovery."

Trish looked at it. "It jus' look like gold."

"And it will be the most important piece of gold that you will ever have for the rest of your prolonged existence. Wear this when you want to be in the sun—when you are full and have no need to feed. Wear this to be human. But take it off to harvest. Take it off to embrace the moon. Take it off to be your true self."

He held her hands in his and looked into her eyes. She wondered what he found. Could he see her soul?

"You are just as important as anything else walking this planet. You are life, an original concept of ancient art and old medical science. But your kind has adapted-shifted."

She couldn't picture moving on from that moment, living a normal life as such a dangerous creature. But what else could she do? *It'll be easier*, she thought. *I can get outta the woods, get a job… Never see Momma again.* She wasn't giving up on herself, and with Ally's serum, anything was possible…except giving up blood. It tasted too good. Even as she stood there sunbathing in the natural glow of the daytime, the thought of how the next stranger would feel her fangs gorge on his blood seeped into her mind. She'd do it, hungry or no. Her teeth nearly gnashed for it. No, to go back to Hopkins meant putting Momma and the town in danger. The town, because Trish would pick them off one by one. Momma would suffer too, having to defend Trish from the allegation of multiple murders because she was her only daughter. Her only kin. Trish was certain that Momma would die for her, and she couldn't have that. There was no going home. Trish could only go forward with what the mysterious man had given her. And as they stood there in the sun, holding hands with a new friend, she couldn't think of anything better.

CHAPTER 40

Paranoia

A prominent ease washed over Trish when she pulled into the driveway, right next to Maggie's Prius. The house looked as peaceful as any other house in the neighborhood. So full of life and memories. Love and disagreements. She learned how easy it was to fit into anyone's home, take part in their normal lives without them knowing her true nature; she learned that lesson early on. It took some real coxing to get Randel to let her move in with him. After a year of dating, he finally caved.

"It's paid off," he'd said over chicken curry. He dragged her to a mom-and-pop Indian Restaurant Downtown Lakeshore. People walked the streets wearing swimming trunks and swimming suits, sweating in the blazing sun. Lake Michigan was just a block away, and summer traffic was at its peak. She had samosas and nervously kept her face as neutral as possible; the garlic coming off his breath was almost unbearable.

"Yeah, but it's your house. Not ours. I was thinking we could look for something together?" Somewhere where she could comfortably hide things. Her apartment was small, but it was full of secrets, stuffed with truths that another pair of eyes could never comprehend. And she'd been to his house before. It was cute, but more space was warranted.

"Ah. I'll just add you to the deed. There. Now you own property too. Trust me, you'll spend more time there than me. You know how work is." He shrugged. "It'll be fine."

"Sure," she responded to the memory. Regardless of the house size or how she came to call it her own, she wanted to run to the front door, rush away from the shit night. But it all felt too easy. After she spent the better half of the last hour cleaning and changing into her yoga clothes, she could finally admit that it was all over. All that was left was the ceremonial burning of any combustible evidence, starting with the dress. She tossed the boots into Grand River on her way back home. She also chucked Barbie's phone, or whatever was left of it, into the rushing waters piece by piece.

Trish cried a little and shouted a lot as she drove, thanks to the mistakes she'd made that could've kept her from home forever. Unlike a lot of people, she didn't get to move on from bad choices or huge mistakes. They stuck around, plaguing all upcoming decisions. She'd never forget, but would forever regret.

Steve had gloated about Trish's existence, glorifying her immortality. But there was nothing unique about being a monster. She watched time go by and bodies pile up. It was a loud, abhorrent noise that she could never turn off. She was doomed, and Steve didn't realize his own luck.

Fully healed, she silently celebrated the onslaught of strength returning to her sore limbs. But the appreciation for her own evolution had seized quickly when an unsettling heat wore on the back of her neck, erecting gooseflesh. She looked over her shoulder, questioning a pair of headlights riding down the street at such a late hour, passing by her home. The car turned into a driveway a few houses down, jogging Trish's memory of her neighbors who had lived there for years. The neighbor's car did indeed belong there.

She sighed; Steve had succeeded in making her nervous. Even after she'd gone about an hour away from Miller, she wanted to accuse her neighbors of watching her when all the houses on the block lay silent. She shivered and slouched in the driver's seat, looking hard and finding nothing. No eyes in any windows, no lights flushing living rooms or bedrooms.

The street slept, leaving her alone in her paranoia.

"Okay," she said, blowing a slow stream of air through her pursed lips. Then she inhaled deeply, filling her chest. "Okay," she whispered to herself again.

Before Darwin, she had had no real purpose. She floated about, collecting accomplishments, all the while existing as she was. But now she may have put Darwin and Randel in serious danger.

No. No, Steve doesn't know where to find me, she reassured. Not only that, but the ring also made her a few shades darker and many years older. She went from a pale, clear-faced, bony nineteen-year-old to a thirty-something riddled with beauty marks, shallow wrinkles, and meaty limbs. Steve wouldn't recognize her underneath her laugh lines or the small crevices along her forehead, or the sacs underneath her eyes.

But if she saw Steve first…

Trish pondered the situation. She had begun the night as usual and ended it with four dead bodies and a deranged enemy.

A dangerously unstable enemy.

But sitting in her Jeep only boosted her fears. She needed to get inside.

Trish cut the engine, grabbed her purse and now-empty duffle bag, and let herself out. She watched the dark windows of her house as it peacefully rested.

The yard was in shadow, and she followed the brick path up to the cement porch. The auto light kicked on, beaming down on her head as she jostled her keys, separating the front door key from the others. Trish shoved the key into the lock and allowed herself inside, just after she'd looked over her shoulder again, finding nothing but darkness and the sleeping residential street she'd grown accustomed to.

It *was* 3:30 a.m., after all.

She imagined pushing the door open and finding Steve inside, holding a gun to Maggie's head, and Darwin—

Stop it, she thought as she opened the door, went inside, and quickly locked it behind her.

Her lips curled and tears threatened to surge. She stood in the foyer and threw her head back. Staring at the dark ceiling, she couldn't help but acknowledge that she'd *been* there before, unsure and terrified. Not for herself—she could deal with Steve. No. For her family. She could never leave the house comfortably until Steve was dead.

Another vampire.

Steve's words stung.

Victoria, she thought.

***

Trish tugged at Maggie's shoulder, waking her with a start.

"Oh, I'm sorry," Maggie said sheepishly, eyes widened as she took in her surroundings.

"It's all right. I know it's late," Trish said. She reached into her purse and pulled her wallet out. Trish presented three hundred-dollar bills that she grabbed at the ATM once she left the river.

Maggie's eyes lit up underneath the sleepy crust around them. Her tiredness morphed into a half-smile. She winced at the dim light in the foyer. Then she sheepishly gathered her phone, backpack, and coat, which had been splayed across the coffee table. "Wow, you don't have to give me this much. It's totally fine."

"I insist," Trish said quietly, preferring Darwin to stay asleep through the night. That way, she could hold him like a teddy bear. She'd kiss and snuggle with him, allowing his essence to make her feel all right.

"Well, thank you. And if you ever need me, just give me a call," Maggie said, stuffing the cash into her coat pocket.

"Thanks, Maggie." Trish followed the girl to the door.

"Have a good night, Mrs. Weston."

Trish gave a half-smile and then watched Maggie cross the walk-way, heading for her car. Quickly, the girl climbed inside, turned on the engine, and took off, probably fighting sleep as she drove.

Trish closed and locked the door after surveying the street again. She killed the foyer light and pulled her phone from her purse to call

Randel. No answer. She didn't bother leaving a message. He always called back.

All things circled Trish's mind, with the most recent events dominating her thoughts.

The last thing Trish wanted was rest.

She also didn't want to revisit Miller, or to be confronted by one of the worst things she'd ever done. Miller University turned out to be Trish's personal hell. It was too close for comfort, and she'd had too many incidents there. All of which happened recently, marking a new personal low.

Once she released herself from the recesses of her stressful mind, Trish found herself standing at Darwin's room door, watching him sleep on his back. She smiled when he twitched a little, wondering if he was dreaming about her talking and playing with him.

Did he dream about her being his mom? Or Randel being his dad?

Tears blurred her vision. Darwin was unlucky, and he'd be better off without her—him *and* Randel. Randel could meet someone else and raise their son with a normal set of parents.

There was no place for Trish in that precious kid's life. She'd only ruin him, just as she'd ruined many others. She—

Trish stopped and peered at the staircase. The grass on the side of the house crackled underneath someone's feet, just outside Darwin's window.

She scowled.

Someone was *lurking* around her house. Trish knew. She could hear quick but heavy steps crushing frosted grass blades. Trish knew it wasn't an animal because they were much lighter and faster than the sounds she was hearing.

No.

Someone was out there.

And someone was going to die.

C H A P T E R 4 1

Existence

Trish rushed, moving quickly as she went to the kitchen, happy to have left the lights out. She drew closer to the intruder, closer to the noise.

This'll be quick, she told herself.

The movements stopped, but she pinpointed the other side of the kitchen wall. Someone was leaning against the house, on the other side of the sink. She listened to him breathe heavily, rocking on his feet, as if waiting.

Trish went over to the knife block and snatched up the butcher's knife. She stepped slowly toward the window next to the counter, ready to throw her blade through the top of the intruder's head as they hid in the shadows of her back yard.

She looked at the knife, then stopped.

All right, Steve, no more messes, she thought, deciding a knife wasn't the tool for the job. Trish dropped it in the sink as another plan formed. She headed for the gun safe deep in her office closet, typed in 092337, and grabbed the pistol.

Trish couldn't make noise at Toby's, but she could protect her home with as much noise as she wanted.

She walked to the patio door, gun cocked and aimed, ready to shoot. She stepped slowly, ready for her finger to slip and blow someone's head open, ready to take a chunk off Steve's skull and declare it self-defense.

How dare you follow me? she thought, her face scorched. She gritted her teeth, cursing herself. Steve was at her home. He knew where her *family* lived.

A soft knock from behind. She spun around and glared.

Someone was at the front door.

Trish narrowed her eyes, baffled. She hadn't heard them move from the back to the front yard. But they were there, at the front door now, wanting her to let them inside.

She sniffed. The air smelled of aftershave, apple juice, and baby formula. There was a hint of sulfur and well water, but nothing out of the ordinary. To be sure, she raced over to the patio door and forced it open, then looked outside.

There was no one crouching or standing where she had heard the noise.

And no unordinary smells. Only foliage.

The knock again.

Trish closed and locked the patio door before trudging to the front.

"Ma'am," a soft-spoken woman on the other side began. "Ma'am, can you please help me?"

Trish didn't say anything. She dropped her weapon and her shoulders. Strange as it was, she decided not to answer. She didn't want to be responsible for hurting whoever the stranger was. Instead, she chuckled to herself.

"Please help me." The woman's frail voice cracked.

Trish didn't reply. There was quiet all around.

Trish flinched when heavy thumps erupted as the woman slammed on the door. "Please! Open the door," she demanded, before letting out an ear-splitting shrill, possibly waking the neighbors. Something metal hit the door as she cried out.

"Stop it, or I will shoot!" Trish yelled, raising the pistol and aiming for the door.

"Ma*ma*!" Darwin screamed from his room.

"Open the door now!" the woman shouted, pounding.

Trish pulled the trigger and watched the bullet tear through the wooden door.

"Ma!" Darwin cried.

"I'm coming, baby," Trish called out, her soul shriveling with each of his cries.

But she held her composure and listened. Darwin screamed, and the pounding had stopped. Trish reached for the door, hoping to find a dead body lying in a pool of blood on her porch. But she couldn't smell blood, which was worrisome.

Trish opened the door and peered down. All she found were wood shavings. There was the yard and her car sitting in the driveway to the right.

And to her left, the bottom of her steel shovel coming fast at her face.

The heavy blow smashed her nose.

The flashes blinded her, and she fell off her feet, back-flopping onto the floor. Pain erupted in her face. She'd heal, but until then, her face was going to sting. Trish was sure her nose was broken.

A thin girl rushed inside and stood before Trish. She kicked the gun; it skittered across the floor and into the kitchen. The frantic girl glared with wet eyes. Trish went to sit up, but the girl put her boot on her chest, forcing Trish down. The weight knocked the wind out of Trish, and she gasped for air.

"Victoria?" Trish mumbled.

"Change me back!" Victoria shouted.

Trish watched the girl, baffled at her strength. Taken by her prowess. She didn't have a scent. Trish *could not* smell Victoria because Victoria wasn't human. She was strong, light on her feet, and clever.

Victoria was… Victoria was…

Making a critical mistake. She took her eyes off Trish and peered toward Darwin's room, where he kept crying, calling for Trish. Crying for Mommy.

Taking the distraction as an opportunity, Trish grabbed Victoria's leg and snatched it, sending her onto the floor next to her.

Victoria grunted when she landed on her side, shaking the floor underneath them on impact. Trish scrambled, but Victoria was just as fast, clawing her way for the kitchen and to the hallway, rushing down the steps once she found her feet.

"No!" Trish yelled, and she charged. Trish knew the girl had gone into Darwin's room.

But Victoria had stopped short of the entrance, only staring at the crying baby.

Catching her breath and shaken with rage, Trish said, "You need to get—"

Victoria cupped her mouth and wailed, never moving her eyes from Darwin. It was as if they were crying together, watching each other's tears flow, both enshrined in shared terror. Before long, Darwin moved his sad eyes to Trish and reached a hand out, wanting comfort, maybe confused about the woman in their home.

While sobbing, Victoria dropped her hand and turned to Trish. "What are you doing with him? Did you steal him?" she shouted.

Trish couldn't answer. She only studied. Victoria Scott's deep bronze skin had gone pale beige, and her cheeks and eyes had sunken. Her face was riddled with dark blemishes, and her hair was thick and matted. Pain sank deep into her once-youthful eyes, and while she cried tears, her mouth hung ajar, showing sharp fangs. She was frail, famished, and too thin to be as strong as she was.

"Answer me!" Victoria demanded.

"I—"

The girl's fangs were sharp and new. Trish couldn't stop staring at them. *Another vampire*, Steve had said.

"Talk!" Victoria said.

"He's mine. My son." Trish held her hands up and moved forward, ready to take the girl down.

"No." Victoria shook her head. "No, that *can't* be true. I know who you are," she said. "I *know* you. People can have babies, not... not monsters." She sobbed. "No... You... I know what you *are*," she growled.

"What are you talking about?" Trish asked calmly.

"You did this to me," Victoria said. "You... I can't... You took my life away from me!" Her voice broke. "You...you *killed* me. And you're going to turn me back. You *have to*."

"I—" Lost for words, Trish could only gleam. How was she... as she was? How come no one other than Steve knew where she'd been? How? How'd she survive the sun? How'd she live in modern times without being reported or caught? Recorded or exposed? How? Trish had over a century of experience, most of which was before technology. *How? How? H—*

"Please. I don't care about what you did tonight or two months ago. Just please. Please, turn me back," Victoria pleaded. "I won't tell anyone. I swear. I just want my life back."

"I—"

Victoria cried. "Please, please. I'll do anything, just... Oh God, I can't do this anymore."

Trish's heart broke for Victoria. She hated the sight but came to terms: there was another body she had to get rid of. But how? Was it even possible?

"Please," the girl wailed, dropping to her knees. "Please. Turn me back." She buried her face in her hands. "I want my old life. I want to eat food. I want my friends. I want...my mom. I want my daddy. I want...I want my life back. Please, please...*turn me back.*"

Darwin watched Victoria as he babbled softly, sharing her pain. Empathy. The boy learned to sympathize.

"Please turn me back, and you'll never see me again. I promise. I won't say anything to the police. I won't. I promise. Just p-please. I-I can't d-do this anymore. *Turn me back.*"

Trish dropped her head and said, "I can't."

EXCERPT FROM
BOOKS 2: MONSTER

PART I

Her

CHAPTER 1

Demands

How dare she? How dare *she?* Trish growled to herself as she stood in her son's, Darwin's, doorway, staring Victoria down. The girl was alive, but not well. She bawled her eyes out as she sat on the floor, her arm draped over the top of Darwin's toy box, and her back settled against the light blue wallpaper. She watched Trish with narrowed eyes, hateful slits full of disdain. Her sunken cheeks may have huffed with her exasperated breaths, but her face looked tight and tired. No longer smooth and youthful, her once brown skin had a gray tint to it.

She looked thirsty.

"Liar," Victoria said, a tight scowl spread across her thinning face.

Blood dripped from Trish's nose after Victoria struck her with the shovel. The throbbing aches in her face were easy to ignore. Instead, Trish imagined choking Victoria to death. Or even shooting her in the face and telling the police that she was a home invader. Trish's feet told her to move, put some plan—any plan—in motion, but her mind demanded that she stayed still.

What if Victoria can't die? Trish thought. *What if choking her doesn't work—what if shooting her doesn't work?* A flash from the past reminded Trish that shooting Victoria would not work and would inevitably result in another failure. Just like Trish failed to end her the night they first met. No. Victoria wasn't dead. She was there, and her fangs were long and sharp, pulling all the attention in the room when she spoke.

Then another thought moved across Trish's mind. If Victoria could die, Trish would have had to kill her in front of Darwin. The uneasy realization made her recoil. She opted to do nothing. Nothing but study.

Victoria's dark, thick hair was pulled back into a low ponytail and her dark brown eyes were wet with tears—no longer hazel as they had been in the photos shared all over the internet, no longer hon-eyed like they were the day Trish had bitten her. Victoria looked frail in her stained light blue hoodie. The stain was a coppery splotch, situated over Victoria's left side. It looked like blood, but Trish wasn't sure. Despite the ring, she should have smelled the blood. But when she sniffed, she smelled nothing of the sort. Alarm tightened her chest. Since when could she not smell blood? Trish made a note to jot the strange phenomena down in her journal right after she'd gotten rid of Victoria. Trish started, "I..." Victoria interrupted, seemingly impatient for a response.

"I know what you are," Victoria said, tears still spilling down her face. "You can play everyone else, but don't pretend like you don't know who I am."

"I'm calling the police," Trish said.

"*Tsk.* No, you won't. You're not stupid."

"I don't know what you're talking about, and you're scaring my son. Leave, or I'll—"

"You are such a *fucking* liar," Victoria quipped. "You might not look as young as you do when you're killing people, but you are a murderer. A *monster*," she said, and when she said it, Trish's gut churned. *A witness.* Trish was so struck by Victoria's existence that she'd forgotten that Victoria did, indeed, know what Trish was.

Victoria shook her head. "Why did you do this to me?"

Trish didn't speak. She took small steps towards Darwin, who, surprisingly, didn't seem upset anymore. He gazed at Victoria from between the wooden rails of his bed, uninterrupted. Victoria didn't seem to care that Trish was moving to shield Darwin. In fact, Victoria didn't seem very scared either, which was baffling to Trish. Victoria knew Trish's true nature, but she didn't flinch or cower. She only talked.

"You destroyed my life when you bit me—when you *killed* me." A pregnant pause, then she wiped her face and pushed herself up to her feet. Her abrupt movement pushed Trish to her final spot just in front of Darwin. She felt his small hands pull on her yoga pants as he groaned and grumbled, as if telling her to move out of the way.

Once Victoria stood, she stopped and looked Trish in the eyes. "But you can change me back. I mean, you look real. You..." She trailed off as her gaze fell onto Trish's belly.

Deny, Trish's thoughts roared. *She needs to leave.* "I don't know what you're talking about. Just, please leave."

Victoria's face crumbled. "Don't talk to me like I'm crazy—I'm not crazy!" she roared.

"Keep your voice down," Trish said through her tightening jaw as she strode towards Victoria, a step away from standing toe to toe with the girl.

"Demons are real..." Victoria muttered as her eyes moved up the length of Trish's body.

No, they're not, Trish thought. "I need you to leave."

But Victoria stood there with pursed lips.

Had she drank anything or anyone—how many bodies has she had? Trish thought.

"I'm not leaving until you change me back."

"Victoria—"

"No! How can you say you don't know what I'm talking about when you somehow know my name? I *saw* you kill Chad!" Her pointed words rolled off her tongue in quick succession.

Trish shuddered. The bodies that she'd left at Miller on different occasions were unquenchable, and the fact that one of those bodies bled over to her front step...

She swallowed as an invisible vise gripped her neck.

Another vampire. Steve's voice.

"I don't know—"

"Patricia Weston," Victoria announced. Trish's name sounded like venom rolling off the scorned girl's tongue. "I know what you are."

Chills shot through Trish's body. Victoria was going to reveal what Trish was if she wasn't handled appropriately and fast. But how could Trish handle her? *How does she know my whole name?* She tried to think of how, but panic stopped her. *One thing at a time. Get... her...out of here.* "So, what are you going to do?" Trish asked, accepting that she'd have to deal with Victoria in another place at another time.

Victoria knitted her brow. "I'm not *doing* anything. You're going to turn me back." She looked over Trish's shoulder and directly at Darwin. "I can't live like this anymore."

"I wish I could help, but I—"

"I can't eat," Victoria said.

Trish tilted her head, wanting to know more.

"I haven't held food down in over two months, and I feel like I'm starving to death." Her voice cracked when she said *death*.

Trish wanted to ask Victoria how she felt. Were their hunger pains alike? But no. Trish said nothing.

"As soon as you change me back, I will leave," Victoria said. She wasn't yelling, but her voice carried. Her proposition boomed in Trish's ears.

Trish thought back to how Victoria ended up in Darwin's room in the first place. She caught Trish off guard with her speed and strength, something that should have been impossible on an empty stomach. *Wow*, Trish thought, encompassed in envy. Victoria wasn't missing anymore; they stood in the same room, and Trish couldn't smell a thing. She sighed.

Victoria stood there for a bit, her breathing getting heavier by the second. "Where are your fangs? Huh?" she finally asked.

"What?" The question caught Trish off guard.

"You used your fangs. I saw them. I felt them."

Trish said nothing.

"You're going to change me back," Victoria demanded.

Darwin cried, and Trish's blood boiled. "You're freaking my kid out! Now leave!"

Victoria frowned at Darwin; a genuine sense of concern crossing her face. Then she looked at Trish, and her face tightened. "I guess you want to make this hard. Okay. I expected that—I mean, why would you help me with anything?" she said facetiously. She walked toward Trish and stopped short, her face blank and wet with drying tears. Her voice shook. "I'll leave, but you *will* change me back."

It sounded more like a desperate plea than an obscure threat.

Trish followed her up the hall and out the front door she had forced her way through. Then she watched Victoria take off, running up the street. She darted, feet barely touching the ground as she sprinted. She was out of sight within seconds.

**Read Trish- A Vampire and Serial Killer
Thriller Series Book 2: Monster today!**

**Sign up for updates, advanced review copies,
and book recommendations from K.T. Rose:**
https://www.kyrobooks.com/subscribe-1

MORE FROM K.T. ROSE

**Trish- A Vampire and Serial
Killer Thriller Series Book 1:
Blood**
*Hunger. Desperation. Terror. A mother's love
knows no bounds - neither does her appetite.*

**Trish- A Vampire and Serial
Killer Thriller Series Book 2:
Monster**
*Blood. Family. Secrets. In the quiet suburbs,
a mother's darkest instincts threaten to
unravel the very foundation of her world.*

**Trish- A Vampire and Serial
Killer Thriller Series Book 3**
Coming January 2026.

Trinity of Horror- Macabre Tales Volume 1
*When suspicion meets desperation, the
inner demons of desperate souls ignite.*

**Netted: A Serial Killer Thriller and
Fast-Paced Suspense Series Box Set Books 1-3**

Netted: A Serial Killer Thiller
and Fast-Paced Suspense
Book 1
The Beginning
Can Dale and Jessica escape Father Paul,
the dark web's most sadistic cult leader?

Netted: A Serial Killer Thiller
and Fast-Paced Suspense
Book 2
Inside Out
Is escape possible from a cult that feeds on fear?

Netted: A Serial Killer Thiller
and Fast-Paced Suspense
Book 3
The Crash
When time runs out, bodies will fall.

Trinity of Horror- Macabre Tales Volume 2
A normal summer day...drenched in blood.

The Haunting of Gallagher Hotel- A
Chilling Haunted House Horror Novel
Pride and greed infect the soul, trapping
the dead in Gallagher Hotel.

Stay connected with K.T. Rose by visiting:
https://www.kyrobooks.com/subscribe-1

Printed in Dunstable, United Kingdom

67214491R00134